Tea and Broken Biscuits

Daphne Neville

Copyright © 2018 Daphne Neville

All rights reserved, including the right to reproduce this book, or portions thereof in any form. No part of this text may be reproduced, transmitted, downloaded, decompiled, reverse engineered, or stored, in any form or introduced into any information storage and retrieval system, in any form or by any means, whether electronic or mechanical without the express written permission of the author.

This is a work of fiction. Names and characters are the product of the author's imagination and any resemblance to actual persons, living or dead, is entirely coincidental.

The views expressed in this work are solely those of the author and do not necessarily reflect the views of the publisher, and the publisher hereby disclaims any responsibility for them.

ISBN: 978-0-244-42826-6

PublishNation
www.publishnation.co.uk

Other Titles by This Author

TRENGILLION CORNISH MYSTERY SERIES
The Ringing Bells Inn
Polquillick
Sea, Sun, Cads and Scallywags
Grave Allegations
The Old Vicarage
A Celestial Affair
Trengillion's Jubilee Jamboree

PENTRILLICK CORNISH MYSTERY SERIES
The Chocolate Box Holiday
A Pasty In A Pear Tree
The Suitcase in the Attic

The Old Tile House

Chapter One

"It's snowing," shrieked Hetty, as she looked from the sitting room window of Primrose Cottage on the last day of February, "Come and see, Lottie. It's real snow like we used to get when we were kids."

Lottie scrambled to her feet from where she was kneeling on the hearth rug stacking logs beside the stove and hastened to the side of her twin sister. Her mouth gaped open in disbelief. "But the sun was shining a few minutes ago. I mean, I know this was forecast but it's changed so quickly."

The sisters sat down on either side of the table beneath the sitting room window and watched as the horizontal snow blew across the landscape from the east, at times so thickly that it completely obscured the distant coastline. Having lived for most of their lives in Northamptonshire they were used to snow where it seemed an every year occurrence during their childhood. However, they were now coming towards the end of their second winter in Cornwall and knew from chatting to their new friends that snow of any magnitude in the county was a rare experience.

Hetty and Lottie were twins; born in 1952 and not looking forward to notching up another year when they reached their next birthday. Lottie was a widow whose husband had died in 2015. Hetty, who was the older of the two by ten minutes, had never married but had devoted her life to her career as a midwife. The sisters had decided to move to Pentrillick in Cornwall during a family holiday in 2016 which they had shared with Lottie's son Bill, his wife Sandra and their three children, Zac, Vicki and Kate. Having made the decision both then sold their respective homes and moved to Primrose Cottage in Blackberry Way the following December.

"Who's that?" Hetty squinted to see if she could make out the huddled figure in the driving snow whose head and shoulders were just visible over the front garden wall.

"It's Kitty." Lottie jumped up when she saw their friend walk between their unlatched garden gates and opened the door before the doorbell rang.

"Come in, come in," Lottie beckoned, "I hope nothing's wrong."

Kitty stamped her feet before she crossed the threshold. She then took off her hat and coat and shook both outside to remove the excess snow. As Lottie closed the door, Kitty hung her outer garments on the newel post at the foot of the stairs and slipped off her wet shoes.

"No everything's fine. I just came to tell you that tonight's drama group meeting is cancelled. Robert put it on the Pentrillick Players' Facebook page but I thought I'd pop round and tell you in person in case you'd not seen it."

"No we hadn't but seeing the weather I'm not surprised." Lottie led Kitty into the sitting room where Hetty had already risen from her seat.

"Coffee, Kitty?" Hetty asked, "You must be frozen."

Kitty blew on her fingers to bring them back to life. "Yes, thank you, that'd be lovely but I've hardly come a long way and the wind was behind me so I got here even quicker than usual."

Kitty and her husband, Tommy, lived in Meadowsweet, the last house along Blackberry Way, a dead-end lane along which eight detached houses enjoyed panoramic views over Pentrillick and the sea beyond.

When the coffee was ready Hetty carried it into the sitting room on a tray. Behind her followed a middle-aged man who held a barrel of biscuits.

"Oh, hello, Sid," said Kitty, surprised to see the plumber, "where did you spring from?"

Hetty placed the mugs on the table. "Sid's been fixing the water. The hot has been running cold since this morning." She shuddered: "it chose to act the fool while I was in the shower."

"Oh dear, what a nuisance. Still, just as well you know a good plumber."

Sid took a bow and placed the biscuit barrel on the table.

"I wholeheartedly agree," said Lottie, "and we really appreciate the fact that he came to our rescue at such short notice."

"You know me," chuckled Sid as he took a seat, "always happy to help out a damsel in distress, or even two."

Seated around the table all four then watched the snow falling, already several inches deep.

"So has Robert decided when the drama group meeting will be?" Lottie asked Kitty.

"Sometime next week. Probably Monday as that's when we usually meet."

"Hmm, shame it wasn't Monday this week because the weather wasn't too bad then," muttered Hetty.

Kitty removed her glasses to prevent the coffee from steaming them up. "But it couldn't be helped, Het. Robert had to go to his parents' Ruby Wedding celebrations and it would have been no good the meeting going ahead without him as he's the best organiser the drama group has ever had."

"Of course, silly me. I'd forgotten that was the reason."

"And what's more," continued Kitty, "he's the only one with a copy of the next play."

"Point taken," chuckled Hetty.

"So are you going to the meeting whenever it is, Sid?" Lottie asked.

"You bet. Making a fool of myself is right up my street. I like a bit of limelight."

"Is that why you were a fortune teller for a while?" Kitty asked, recalling his stint as Psychic Sid.

"Hmm, yes and no. Psychic Sid was a bit of a whim and I enjoyed it while it lasted but there's only so much you can read into folk's fortunes," he chuckled, "or make up as the case was with me."

Kitty smiled. "At least you're honest and I'm glad you're joining us as we're usually a bit short of men."

"So will your Tommy be going to the meeting whenever it is?" Lottie asked.

Kitty shook her head. "No, amateur dramatics isn't really Tommy's thing. Although he always supports the performances and helps out with scenery if there's a shortage of willing helpers. I'm so glad you've all decided to join the drama group this year. It's great fun and I'll be able to walk down to the meetings with you ladies."

"And you can pop into the Crown and Anchor on the way home afterwards," said Sid. "I've noticed most of the group do."

Lottie broke a biscuit in half and dipped it in her coffee. "I like the idea of that."

"Yes, as Sid said quite a few members make a beeline for the pub," admitted Kitty, "even those who don't pass it on their way home. It's a nice way to round off the evening especially if rehearsals are going well."

"I must confess I'm quite looking forward to it all," said Hetty as she glanced at the fire and saw that it was burning low, "Last year's production was extremely good and I was very impressed." She stood up and put another log on the fire.

"Yes, there's quite a lot of talent in the village," agreed Kitty as she placed her empty mug down on the table and put her glasses back on, "and I think the arrival of Brett Baker will bring a lot more people out of the woodwork - out of curiosity if for no other reason."

Brett Baker was a playwright and writer of popular situation comedies, several of which had been televised over the years. He had first appeared in Pentrillick in January when it became apparent to those who felt it their duty to keep the villagers up to date with the local news, that he was the new owner of Sea View Cottage, a property which for several years had been a holiday let. Shortly after his arrival in the village, Brett was introduced by Ashley Rowe, the landlord of the Crown and Anchor, to Robert Stephens who was the brains behind the village's amateur dramatic society. The two got along well which resulted in Brett offering Robert, free of charge, a play he had written some time ago which had never been performed anywhere. Robert accepted with enthusiasm and promised the play would be the next production of the Pentrillick Players in late May.

"So, what's Brett Baker's play about?" Lottie asked.

Kitty shook her head. "I've not the foggiest idea. Robert's playing it very close to his chest."

Hetty finished her coffee and took a quick glance out of the window. The snow had eased and visibility was much improved. "Well, I suppose it's only fair that everyone gets to know the details at the same time."

Kitty nodded. "I think that is the general idea. So will you be hoping for a part in the play or will you be volunteering for backstage chores?"

"I'll do whatever is deemed necessary," chuckled Hetty, "I mean if there is a part for a lady the wrong side of sixty then I may well go for it."

Lottie looked aghast. "Backstage for me. I'll be offering to help with the costumes."

"I share your sentiments, Lottie," Kitty smiled. "Playing the piano is as near as you'd ever get me to performing."

Sid stood. "I'd best make my way home now in case the weather gets any worse. Thanks for the coffee and biscuits, ladies and if I don't see you before, I'll see you at the meeting."

Later in the day the snow showers were less frequent and so when the sun put in an appearance, Hetty pulled on her boots and walked out into the back garden to take pictures on her phone. The fresh snow crunched beneath her feet as she made her way along the curved garden path; her fingers crossed that she did not misjudge the location of paving slabs and tread on any precious plants. Near to the holly bush, the heads of daffodils battered by the wind hung from their broken stems; Hetty carefully picked off the damaged flowers and bunched them together, she then continued along the path. By the pond she paused, the only reminder of its existence were the recognisable leaves of plants peeping up through the snow. She trod carefully to avoid standing on the ice and laughed when she saw the two foot tall decoy plastic heron which wore a fluffy white coat. Hetty felt sorry for the fish hidden beneath the snow covered sheet of ice but knew they would survive well enough as long as the cold spell lasted no more than a few days. She also took comfort from the fact they were at least safe from any herons which might not be fooled by their motionless plastic relative in his white winter coat. After taking several pictures she returned indoors and placed the damaged daffodils on the kitchen window sill in a ceramic vase.

There was no more snow during the night but the following morning the temperature was still well below freezing. Hetty was up first and when she attempted to fill the kettle, no water gushed from the tap.

"Great. Frozen pipes." However, she was not too concerned for having lived alone for most of her adult years she was used to fending for herself. From a drawer in the sideboard she took out her hairdryer and then slipped on her boots. From the garage she fetched an extension wire and then clothed only in nightdress and dressing gown she warmed the pipe until she heard a hiss and knew the water was flowing again.

Back in the warm, Hetty made a mug of tea then dropped two slices of bread into the toaster and because they were the last two slices, she went to the freezer to take out another loaf. There was no bread in the freezer.

Hetty slammed shut the freezer door. "Humph! It's going to be one of those days."

Ten minutes later, Lottie appeared showered, dressed and cheerful. "Morning, Het," her shoulders slumped when she saw her sister's glum face. "What's up?"

"No bread in the freezer and I've just used the last two slices."

"Oh well, we'll just have to pop down to the village and hope the shop has some. It'd be nice to get outside for a while anyway and Albert could do with a walk."

The walk down Long Lane was a little hair-raising; the road had not been gritted and so it was icy where cars had travelled to and fro. To maintain their dignity the sisters kept to the side of the road and walked on undisturbed snow which crunched noisily beneath their feet. Albert, Hetty's Jack Russell terrier, however, refused to tread on the cold white stuff and so Hetty had to carry him until they reached the village at the bottom of the hill where the pavements along the main street had been cleared.

The village was unusually quiet. Very few cars drove along the road and only two or three pedestrians walked along the pavements. But inside the post office, several people were gathered merrily exchanging tales about the weather.

"Hello," gushed a cheery voice as Hetty took one of the last three loaves from the shelf, "is everything okay with you?"

"Yes, thank you, Emma: apart from the fact we've run out of bread," said Lottie.

"And the pipes were frozen this morning," groaned Hetty as she dropped the loaf into the wire basket.

Lottie took a bag of flour and dried yeast sachets from the shelf so that she could make bread should the bad weather continue and supplies run out. "I suppose you're all perky because the college is closed today."

"Yes, that and the fact we don't see snow very often. When I get home, Claire and I are going to build a snowman." The rosy cheeks, and green eyes sparkling beneath her striped woollen hat, made Emma looked younger than her nineteen years.

"Claire?" Lottie queried.

"My little sister."

"Yes, of course."

"No doubt there will be a lot of snowmen and excited children around with the schools closed," chuntered Hetty, "although I don't recall them ever closing when we were kids; yet I remember we had some awful winters back in Northants, especially in 1963."

"Health and safety," blurted Lottie, as she took a jar of coffee from the shelf, "I'm sure that's why they close today at the drop of a hat."

Emma smiled broadly. "Talking of Northants, I hear you have the family coming down this Easter."

Lottie laughed. "Yes, and I suppose Zac told you."

"That's right he did. I can't wait to see him again and it'll be nice to see the rest of the family too."

"I must admit we're quite excited. We've not seen any of them apart from Zac since we moved here to Cornwall and it'll be nice to have our loft conversion used."

"Well, I hope the weather's a lot better than this for Easter," said Emma, glancing out of the window, "or we'll spend most of the holiday huddled by the fire."

After they left the shop, the sisters walked down to the deserted beach. The tide was in and to their delight the sand and shingle were completely hidden beneath a thick blanket of snow except where the waves had splashed onto the shore.

"Not even any seagulls here today," observed Lottie as she made a snowball and tossed it into the sea. The sisters watched, mesmerised as the snowball bobbed about until it was finally washed onto the shore, still intact.

"Brrr, it's too cold to hang around here," muttered Hetty, rubbing her gloved hands together, "let's go home and put the kettle on."

Early that evening before Hetty drew the curtains she looked to the heavy pale grey skies. Beneath it the distant horizon was blurred and once again thick snow was blowing horizontally from the east on an ever increasing wind. "Well," she whispered as she pulled the curtains together, "March has certainly come in like a lion. Let's hope the old proverb is right and it goes out like a lamb."

Chapter Two

Overnight strong winds battered the area but as temperatures rose above freezing and rain fell, the snow began to melt and by daylight most of it had gone.

"Hurrah," sang Hetty, as she pulled back the sitting room curtains, "back to normal now. Spring is just round the corner so I think I'll sow some seeds."

"But it's still very cold, Het. I should wait awhile."

"Well no, because I'm thinking of sowing chillies and they're very slow growing so it'll be ages before they're ready for the greenhouse."

"I didn't know you had any chilli seeds."

"Yes, I have. I bought some at the car boot sale last year because I like the shape of them and the name. They're called Scotch Bonnets."

"Scotch Bonnets!" laughed Lottie. "My Hugh loved making curries but he wouldn't use them because they were too hot."

"No, can't be that bad. I'm sure they'll be fine."

"On your head be it."

On Monday evening, the Pentrillick Players held the meeting postponed from the previous week. Hetty and Lottie walked down to the village with Kitty, all eagerly looking forward to hearing details of Brett Baker's play. As they approached the village hall a steady stream of people were going inside and the three ladies agreed it looked as though there was going to be a very good turnout.

Robert Stephens began the meeting by apologising for the cancellation of the previous meeting but said had it gone ahead it was unlikely many would have ventured out in the atrocious conditions. Several heads nodded while others voiced their agreement. Robert then proceeded to recap on the previous year's performance during which he read out a glowing report from a local newspaper in case there was anyone present who had missed it.

"Oh, come on, Robert," blurted Tess Dobson, as he lay down the newspaper, "cut the waffle and tell us what this play's about. That's what we're all dying to know." Tess was seated on the end of the front row and determined not to miss any facts worthy of repeating to whoever might be willing to listen.

Robert chuckled as he cast his eyes over the gathered crowd in rows, overlooked by the stern faces of deceased members of past village hall committees whose framed pictures hung around the walls of the old hall. Most in attendance were ladies and many he had never met before. In fact, in the fifteen years he had been the organiser of the Pentrillick Players' performances he had never seen such a large crowd at a first meeting and he was very much aware of the reason for the turnout.

"It's a comedy and a murder mystery," said Robert, "and as usual it's a three act play and most of the action takes place in the drawing room of a large country house owned by a celebrity hair stylist and his wife."

One of the ladies raised her hand. "Well, if you need any help with hairdressing and suchlike then Karen and I are your girls. We both work in the salon here in the village." The person seated beside her nodded vigorously.

"Now that is interesting, and you are?"

"Nicki, Nicki Timmins."

"And I'm Karen Walker."

"Thank you Nicki and Karen I'm sure your contribution will be invaluable and may I say welcome to our drama group. In fact

I must extend the welcome to all the new faces. I don't think I've ever seen such a good turnout for a first meeting."

Someone coughed.

"Oh yes, and of course a big welcome to the old familiar faces as well."

"Less of the old," chided Daisy, who worked in the village charity shop.

Robert chuckled. "Come on, Daise, you know what I meant."

Taffeta, a young attractive blonde who ran and worked in Taffeta's Tea Shoppe, raised her hand as though still at school. "Robert, sorry to interrupt but what we all want to know is: is Brett Baker coming here tonight?"

Most of the ladies nodded and uttered words of agreement.

"No, not tonight because he went up to London this afternoon." There was a collective groan. "But I can assure you that at some time during rehearsals he will be showing his face and he hopes to keep track of our progress over the coming months."

There was much excitement amongst the ladies and even some of the men. Brett Baker, the professional playwright who had recently bought Sea View Cottage, and was the author of the play for their next performance, was after all the reason for the large turnout. For many saw themselves as leading ladies and men who would receive gushing praise from the village's newest and most prestigious inhabitant.

During the next hour, Robert gave a few more details to the meeting about the nature of the play and the proposed dates for performances but he refrained from revealing who any of the characters were including the status of the murder victim and his/her assassin for he wanted members to read the play and find out for themselves. He ended the meeting by saying he was in the throes of printing off scripts and once done he would leave copies in the post office so that anyone interested in auditioning for a part the following Monday could familiarise themselves with the script. The meeting was adjourned at nine o'clock.

"Crown and Anchor?" Kitty asked Hetty and Lottie as she picked up her handbag.

Hetty chuckled. "Do you need to ask?"

"No, but then again you might have been fancying an early night."

"Not likely. I'm brimming with enthusiasm and can't wait to get my hands on a copy of the script."

"And hoping no doubt that one of the characters will be a lady on the wrong side of sixty." Lottie buttoned up her coat and pulled on a pair of woollen gloves. "Come on, let's go before everyone else gets there and the seats by the fire have all been taken."

The three ladies were first to get to the pub and so were able to claim the table nearest the log fire. Shortly after they had bought drinks and were seated, Alex and Ginny, who lived next door to Hetty and Lottie, arrived and asked if they might join them.

"Of course," said Lottie, moving around on the cushioned bench.

"We were just saying how keen we are to read the play through," gushed Hetty. "It sounds quite exciting."

Ginny put down her glass and removed her scarf. "It does, I just hope it doesn't upset the Liddicott-Treens. They've been patrons of the drama group for years and do a lot to help."

Hetty frowned. "But why on earth would they be upset by an amusing murder mystery play?"

"Because the setting is in a large country house and the burglary episode might bring back bad memories of the robbery," said Alex.

Kitty's hands flew to her mouth. "Oh, my goodness, I hadn't thought of that. Someone will have to warn them to soften the blow."

Lottie took a large sip of wine. "Would you care to enlighten us a bit because Het and I have no idea what you're talking about?"

"No, I suppose you wouldn't," agreed Ginny, "it must be two or three years ago now since it happened so before your time."

"And the rest," gushed Kitty, "Jeremy and Jemima were still at the village primary school back then and they're both well into their teens now."

"I think it was 2013," said Alex, his brow knitted as he thought, "and it was about this time of year. Well no, actually it would have been a bit earlier than this because it was half term."

"So five years. Yes, that sounds about right." Kitty nearest the fire, stood up and removed her coat.

Hetty drummed her fingers on the table. Lottie tapped her feet.

Ginny laughed. "Alex, Kitty, is it just me or do you also detect a look of impatience on the faces of the ladies from Primrose Cottage?"

Kitty tried not to giggle. "Sorry, we got a bit carried away with minutiae there." She looked at Ginny and Alex. "Shall I tell them about it or will you?"

"You can do it and we'll prompt you if you miss a bit or get it wrong," said Ginny.

"Okay," She turned to face Hetty and Lottie. "Well, as you've already guessed it happened during half term week in 2013 when Tristan, Samantha and the two children were away on holiday abroad somewhere or other: *it*, of course being the robbery. While the Liddicott-Treens were away the house and grounds were as usual open to the public during the day but because they were away it was the responsibility of the staff to lock up at night and set the burglar alarms. On the Friday night before the family were due to return home, thieves broke into the house and stole two seventeenth century pistols, a solid silver platter worth a lot of money and jewellery which had been in the Liddicott-Treen family for many, many years which was extremely valuable from a money point of view and also sentimentally." Kitty paused, "Was there anything else?"

Ginny shook her head. "No, I don't think so."

"There was," corrected Alex, "you've forgotten the Fabergé eggs. I believe there were two of them."

Kitty gasped. "Of course, how could I have forgotten them; they were absolutely exquisite."

"But surely things of such value weren't just left lying around the house. I mean, that's asking for trouble," spluttered Hetty.

Lottie nodded. "Quite right. It should all have been locked up in the safe."

Alex smiled. "Well, to be fair none of it was just lying around. In fact quite the opposite, it was all in a very secure room with no windows and a door with several complex locks."

"And everything that was taken was kept in locked display cases for visitors who toured the house to see and because I'd seen them often, that's how I know the Fabergé eggs were exquisite," Kitty added.

Ginny nodded enthusiastically. "And there was always a security guard on duty when people were touring the house."

"Humph, well none of it could have been very secure if thieves got in," scoffed Hetty.

"They were professionals, Hetty," said Alex, "they deactivated the alarms and blew open the secure door with explosives. Of course had it not been for Pickle the poacher who was fishing on the lake knowing there was no-one in the house, the robbery might not have been discovered until the next morning when the staff arrived. As it was Pickle phoned the police on his mobile and raised the alarm because he saw flashlights and was aware of a vehicle in the grounds."

Ginny sighed. "Such a shame he didn't spot the lights earlier though because if he had the thieves might have been caught red-handed: as it was they had gone before the police arrived."

Hetty frowned. "Would it be a silly question to ask who Pickle is?"

"Obviously a poacher," sighed Lottie, "that's what Alex just said."

"Yes, I gathered that but who is he and why is he called Pickle?"

Kitty smiled. "His real name is Percy Pickering but when he was little he couldn't say Pickering and so called himself Percy Pickling. That caused several people to call him young Pickling and it gradually got shortened to Pickle."

"And he lives in one of the council houses along Hawthorn Road," said Ginny, "Except the house doesn't belong to the council now because Percy and his wife bought it several years back. Sadly though his wife is no longer with us because she died two or three years ago. They have a couple of grown up sons but neither one lives in the village now. One is in Falmouth and the other in Taunton."

"And if you want some gardening jobs done he's the chap to call," suggested Kitty, with enthusiasm, "A lot of people, especially the elderly, swear by him and his rates are very reasonable. Not that I'm suggesting either of you are elderly or need help."

"Thank you, Kitty. We'll bear that in mind because I must admit sometimes the heavy jobs can be a bit much." Lottie made a mental note to write down Percy Pickering when she got home.

"He must be a bit trustworthy then," reflected Hetty, "and I hope he wasn't prosecuted for trespassing and poaching."

"He wasn't," Alex confirmed.

"So did the police ever catch the thieves?" Lottie asked.

Ginny shook her head. "Sadly not. They got clean away."

Hetty tutted. "And what about the stolen goods. Were they ever recovered?"

"No, none of them; as Samantha used to say, it all seems to be lost without trace." Ginny tutted as she picked up her glass of wine and took a large gulp.

"And they never had any real leads as to who the robbers might have been," added Kitty, "and everyone in the village was questioned, even holiday-makers down for half term."

Alex half-smiled. "Yes, we all had to provide an alibi. Especially Ginny and me having an interest in antiques."

"What!" Lottie exclaimed, "I mean, surely they never suspected you two."

"They did," laughed Ginny, "It was quite funny really."

"And silly too," scoffed Kitty, "as I'm sure whoever the thieves were they were miles away from Pentrillick long before the investigation got underway."

Alex agreed. "Yes, and I recall the police were mystified that there was not a shred of evidence to link the thieves to the crime. Which ratifies my earlier claim that it was done by professionals."

"Who no doubt sussed out the security system at some point while viewing the house as tourists," said Lottie.

Alex nodded. "Precisely."

"Don't they have CCTV?" Hetty asked.

Ginny shook her head. "No, at least they didn't back then but they do now in parts of the house where it's deemed necessary."

Hetty sighed. "Well I can see your point about not wanting the Liddicott-Treens offended although I'm sure the robbery in Brett's play will be nothing like as dramatic."

"I hope not," grinned Alex, "and I must admit I'm looking forward to reading it."

"Me too," gushed Hetty.

"Out of interest, have either Tristan or Samantha ever taken part in any of the productions?" Lottie asked.

"No," said Ginny, "but a couple of years back they let us rehearse at Pentrillick House because Paul who was very talented and our leading man that year couldn't make rehearsals on the group's usual night which is Monday because he often went up-country for long weekends, so we opted for Tuesday instead but then of course we couldn't use the village hall because it's bingo night."

"And we had the performance at a different time of year as well," added Alex, "Because Paul couldn't spare the time in May, we went for September."

"So is this Paul still around?" Hetty felt he was not someone she had encountered before.

Ginny shook her head. "Sadly not. He was only here for six months and left at the end of September."

"I see, so he would have left shortly before Lottie and I moved down here."

Kitty frowned. "Wasn't he in the Navy or something like that?"

"Possibly," Alex replied, "Someone certainly claimed to have seen him in a uniform one day but I don't know how reliable that person is or even who it was. Rumour had it that he was down here for training purposes, something along those lines. He never talked about work at all but then I suppose they're not allowed to. You know, official secrets and all that."

Hetty chuckled. "Cloak and dagger stuff, eh?"

"I don't think he was in the Navy," remarked Ginny, "because he was often around during the day so I reckon he worked from home and was probably a novelist incognito or something like that."

"How exciting, "declared Lottie, "So out of interest where did he live while he was here?"

"He rented one of the houses in the terrace up near the Vicarage," said Ginny.

"Married?" Hetty asked.

Ginny laughed. "I don't know and as I said he was only here for six months."

"And if he was married his wife wasn't down here with him," divulged Kitty, "but I do recall he had quite a few women keen to make his acquaintance."

Chapter Three

On Wednesday morning, Hetty calmly announced that she was taking Albert for a walk down to the village and asked Lottie if she'd like to join her. Lottie declined saying she wanted to make a start on the sweater she proposed to knit for her son Bill, so that it would be ready when he and the family arrived for Easter. Hetty was quite happy with that because the real reason for her walk to the village was to visit the post office to see if Robert had yet dropped off copies of the play. However, her curiosity was resolved even before she reached the post office for she met Tess Dobson flicking through sheets of A4 paper as she walked along the pavement.

"Is that the play?" Hetty eagerly asked.

"Yes, and if you want a copy you better get there quick because according to Gail, Robert dropped off sixty copies this morning but there are only half a dozen left now."

Hetty gasped. "Really! Thanks, Tess, I'll put my skates on. Come on, Albert, best foot forward." And with a quick wave to Tess she hurried off as fast as Albert's short legs could go.

"So what's it called?" Lottie asked, as her sister arrived back at Primrose Cottage waving the penultimate copy of the play.

Hetty quickly unhooked the lead from Albert's collar and removed her coat. "*Murder at Mulberry Hall*," she gabbled as she kicked off her shoes and tossed them into the cupboard beneath the stairs.

"Hmm, not the most imaginative of names."

"No, I suppose not but then it's easy to remember."

"And self-explanatory."

Hetty sat down heavily on the settee and put on her slippers. "I'm feeling quite breathless. Albert and I practically ran up Long Lane."

Lottie tutted. "But there's no rush to read it. There are still five more days until the next meeting."

"But the next meeting will be the auditions so it's imperative I get to know the play inside out before then."

"So are any of the characters on the wrong side of sixty?"

"That my dear, Lottie, is what I'm about to find out. Meanwhile, would you be a sweetheart and make your poor old sister a mug of coffee?"

Lottie laid down her knitting and stood up. "Of course. It's not every day that I get the chance to make coffee for a rising celebrity."

"Cheeky," chortled Hetty, "Anyway, the characters are probably all young and glamorous."

"Humph, won't be very realistic then if they are."

When Lottie returned from the kitchen with two mugs of coffee she found her sister beaming.

"I've just read through the list of characters and there are several parts for ladies of my age. Well, ladies nearly my age anyway. Shall I read the list to you?"

Lottie sat down. "Please do."

"Well, there are seventeen parts all told but I daresay some of them will have next to nothing to say. The main characters seem to be a hairstylist and his wife who are both in their forties or fifties, a detective inspector of a similar age, a police sergeant around thirtyish and the hairstylist's daughter in her twenties. Then there are friends staying for the weekend of a similar age to the protagonists and a journalist who calls to interview the hairstylist for an article in a glamour magazine and the hairstylist's mother-in-law who's in her sixties or seventies."

"Ah, so you could be the mother-in-law."

"Well, yes, but I'm thinking more along the lines of the hairstylist's wife. I know she's in her forties or fifties but the audience wouldn't be close enough to see any wrinkles would they? And I don't really have that many anyway so I'm sure I could get away with it."

"Hmm possibly. So who are the rest?"

"Well, there's also a housemaid but she's in her teens. Then there's a cook in her sixties and a gardener and a housekeeper both in their forties or fifties and finally there are four SOCO people with no age reference but then I suppose they could be any age as they'll be covered from head to toe in those big white suits they wear."

"SOCOs," repeated Lottie, "what on earth are SOCOs?"

Hetty tutted loudly. "Oh, come on, Lottie. SOCO means Scenes of Crime Officers. You get them in all television crime drama; they're the clever Dicks."

"Yes, of course." Lottie placed her empty coffee mug on the floor and picked up her knitting. "So, who gets murdered?"

"Now that I have yet to establish. I'll read it through and tell you when I know. Reading it will also help me decide who I'd like to be."

An hour later Hetty laid down the sheets of paper and sat tapping her fingers against her chin.

"What's up, Het? Don't you like the idea of playing the wife of a hairstylist?"

Hetty wrinkled her nose. "Yes and no. I mean, she sounds alright but rather snooty and a bit boring. I think I might go for the cook instead."

"Much better idea," agreed Lottie, "at least you're the right age if she's in her sixties."

"Which of course, she is. The part appeals though because it's the cook who gets murdered." Hetty chuckled and wrung her hands.

"Really. So does the murder take place on stage or is it just referred to?"

"It takes place on stage. The hairstylist is away for the night at a conference and his wife has gone to stay with friends and both are due back the following day. The cook is the only person in the house because neither the maid nor the housekeeper live in. In the middle of the night, a burglar comes onto the stage and places explosives on the safe door. The muffled noise of the small explosion brings in the cook to investigate. She sees the burglar emptying the safe and screams. The burglar turns, grabs a candlestick and whacks her over the head with it and she falls to the floor. The burglar does a runner with the valuables and the gardener who lives in a cottage in the grounds having heard the scream runs onto the stage where he finds the poor cook in a heap on the floor."

Lottie laughed. "I see, so for part of the play you'd be a corpse."

"Yes, which suits me fine. I mean, I'd be on stage and the centre of attention but wouldn't have to say anything."

"So which of the characters is the burglar?"

"The hairstylist's wife. The friends she is staying with live in a big bungalow so when they've gone to bed she creeps out of their home in the middle of the night and returns to Mulberry Hall where she breaks into her own house and blows open the safe. Of course it's easy for her to slip out of the bungalow because the rooms are all at ground level and no-one suspects her because she has the perfect alibi."

"So why does she break into her own safe?" Lottie was confused.

"Because her husband's business isn't really making enough money to pay for the lifestyle they lead so it's done in order to claim on the insurance."

"I see, so he's in on it too?"

"Yes, and being at the conference he also has an alibi."

"So the cook is murdered by a woman?"

"Correct."

"I wonder who'll get that part."

"Time will tell but it won't matter anyway if I don't get to play the cook."

"So does the cook have much to say prior to her death?"

"Not a great deal which is ideal because my memory isn't as good as it used to be."

Over the next few days Hetty repeatedly practised lines spoken by Mrs Appleby the cook in varying accents so that she would be ready for the auditions on Monday and she asked Lottie for her opinion.

"I think," said Lottie, much amused, "that it might be best if you stuck to normal English. Your Yorkshire accent is quite good but if I'm honest, the Scottish, Cornish, Cockney and Irish are all terrible."

"What about the Welsh?"

Lottie laughed. "I didn't even realise you'd attempted Welsh."

Chapter Four

On Monday morning, Chloe, who ran Tuzzy-Muzzy, a guest house next door to Primrose Cottage, walked along the main street of the village beneath her umbrella on the way back from the hairdressers. As she passed Sea View Cottage, she saw Brett Baker outside taking items from the boot of his car and with him was his girlfriend, Alina, who rumour had it was an actress. Chloe hurried home keen to relay the news to fellow members of the drama group on social media; she arrived home in Blackberry Way just as Hetty was leaving Primrose Cottage with Albert on his lead.

"It looks like Brett's back in the village," said Chloe, taking down her umbrella for the rain had eased a little, "I've just seen him with his girlfriend. At least I assume she's his girlfriend."

"I've heard she's tall and slim with long blonde hair."

"Yes, that sounds like her."

Hetty groaned. "Oh dear, that's not good then because it means they might be at tonight's meeting."

"That's what I'm thinking and I'm quite nervous enough about auditioning without Brett being there with his actress girlfriend."

"Me too," Hetty felt her heart thumping, "and I suppose it's just as well to be forewarned because we can only do our best."

"You're right, and for that reason I intend to warn everyone I know who is after a part in case they've not heard."

"So what part are you going after, Chloe?"

"The housekeeper. I don't want a big part because as the season moves on I'll be busy with the guest house. Besides, I'm not very gifted when it comes to acting but I love being involved. How about you, Het?"

"I've given it quite a bit of thought and have decided I'll be most suited to play Mrs Appleby, the cook, so I shall try for that."

"Good choice, I hope you get it."

"Thanks, Chloe. Hope you get the part you want too."

"Thanks, anyway, see you later."

"Yes, 'bye."

When Hetty and Albert arrived back from their walk, Hetty sowed some tomato seeds and placed them by the radiator to germinate. Lottie picked up the seed packet which was empty.

"Have you sowed them all?"

"Yes, and I know there were quite a few in there but I expect most will fail as they're old seeds which I brought with me from Northants."

"I think you might be in for a surprise." Lottie crossed over to the window and peeped outside. "I see the rain's stopped so I think I'll drive down to Penzance to get some more wool. Do you want to come?"

"Not really, I got a bit damp while out walking so don't really want to venture out again."

"Okay, I won't be long anyway because I know just what I want."

"Why do you need more wool? I thought you bought some the other day."

"I did for Bill's sweater but somehow I managed not to buy enough and I must get it finished by the time they arrive for Easter."

"Not like you, you're usually pretty good at stuff like that."

"Yes, I think I must have read it wrong. Probably because I wasn't wearing my reading glasses at the time."

Hetty tutted. "Okay, off you go then and drive carefully."

"I will. Bye, Het."

As the car pulled out of the driveway Hetty sat down by the fire with Albert at her feet and read *Murder at Mulberry Hall* yet again. When she finished she laid the script down on the hearth rug and leaned back in the armchair. "Oh Albert, I'd really love to be Mrs Appleby, she sounds like fun. Please wish me well for tonight because I think I'll need all the luck in the world."

As Albert looked up having heard mention of his name, they heard a timid knock on the front door.

"I wonder who that is," Hetty muttered, rising to her feet.

On opening the door she was surprised to see an elderly lady with grey hair pulled back tightly in a ponytail. She was a little over five feet tall and wore a long black coat with a thick knitted shawl draped over her shoulders. Hanging from her arm was a wicker basket. From it she took a sprig of dried flowers. "Want to buy some lucky heather, dear?" she asked.

"Lucky," Hetty repeated.

"Yes, *very* lucky." The elderly lady's smile revealed a row of gleaming teeth.

Hetty looked at the sprig of white heather gripped between the fingers of the old lady's woollen gloves. "Well, yes, actually I might. How much?"

"One pound, dear."

"Well, you just wait here while I get my purse." Hetty ran indoors and grabbed her purse from her handbag. "Here you are." She placed a one pound coin in the woman's outstretched hand who in return gave her the sprig of heather.

"Thank you, my dear. May good luck be yours always." She dropped the coin into her pocket and turned to walk away.

"Just a minute," called Hetty, feeling sorry for the elderly lady, "It's cold out there: would you like a cup of tea? I was just going to make one."

"That would be lovely. Thank you, dear."

Hetty led the woman into the sitting room and offered her a chair by the fire. "I won't be a minute. I'll just put the kettle on."

As she went out to the kitchen she heard a car pull up outside. Lottie was back.

"Tea," called Hetty, as she heard the front door open and then close.

"Yes, thanks." As Lottie took off her jacket and hung it on a peg in the hallway she glimpsed sight of the visitor through the open sitting room door. "Who on earth is that?" she whispered as she walked into the kitchen and dropped her bag of wool on the work surface.

"Er, well I don't actually know her name but she's selling lucky heather so I bought a sprig because I could do with some luck to help me with tonight's auditions."

"But…but." Lottie was speechless.

"If you're worried she might be dishonest go and keep an eye on her. I thought she looked cold so I'm making her a cup of tea and it's nearly ready now."

Lottie went into the sitting room and took a seat opposite the elderly lady who sat beside the fire. She half smiled. "Hello, my name's Lottie. What's yours?"

"Lucy. Would you like to buy a sprig of lucky heather, dear?" Lucy looked hopeful as she pointed to her basket.

Lottie took in a deep breath. "No thank you. I'm not superstitious."

Hetty entered the room carrying a tray; from it she took three mugs and placed them on the coffee table along with the barrel of biscuits. "Sugar?" she asked.

Lucy shook her head. "No, thank you, dear."

Hetty handed her a mug of tea. "Please help yourself to biscuits."

"That's very kind. Thank you."

Hetty took a biscuit and sat down on the settee.

"Break it in half," ordered Lucy, before Hetty took a bite.

"What? Why?"

"Break it and lay the two halves on the plate and then I will tell your fortune."

The shock caused Lottie to slurp her tea.

Hetty broke the biscuit and passed the plate to Lucy who sucked her teeth noisily. "Hmm, I can see by the shape where the biscuit is broken that there will be much drama in your life over the coming months and I don't just mean with the play."

Hetty gasped. "How do you know about the play?"

Lottie nodded to the script lying on the floor.

"So what's going to happen?" Hetty was intrigued.

"I see yellow tulips in a shaft of sunlight. I see a lady cooking and she will get hurt. Other people will get hurt. Some will be deceitful. Things will go missing. Nothing will make sense." She smiled, "But you, dear lady shall be unhurt for the lucky heather will protect you and your family."

"And you can tell all that from the edges of broken biscuits," smirked Lottie. She wanted to laugh out loud but thought it wise to be cautious just in case Lucy did have a smidgen of mystic powers.

Lucy passed the plate back to Hetty. "Now you must eat the biscuit, dear."

Hetty did as she was asked.

"Would you like me to do a biscuit reading for you now, dear?" Lucy asked Lottie.

"Err, no thank you, I'm not hungry."

The three ladies then drank their tea in silence.

"Well, you do pick 'em," said Lottie, as they stood on the doorstep and waved goodbye to their unusual guest, "I mean, broken biscuits. How ridiculous. Whatever happened to reading good old fashioned tealeaves?"

"Teabags," Hetty closed the door. "But you must admit, Lottie, that what she said is quite unnerving. I mean, how does she know that Mrs Appleby the cook in the play gets murdered?"

Lottie laughed. "She didn't say murdered, Het, she said hurt. Anyway, I expect while you were making the tea she took a quick peek at your script and saw the cook got a knock on the head. Had she had the time to look further she'd have found out the blow was fatal and then said murdered instead of hurt."

Hetty picked up her sprig of heather. "Well whatever, I'm not going to leave the house without this in future."

Lottie decided not to comment but instead said, "I wonder where she lives. I've not seen her before."

"Me neither, but I shall ask around at tonight's auditions to see if she paid anyone else a visit."

"Good idea. If anyone knows, Tess will."

As feared by Hetty and Chloe, Brett and Alina were both at the meeting on Monday evening. There were a lot of nervous faces.

"I wasn't expecting him to be here tonight," groaned Marlene, a school dinner lady. "I mean, I wanted him to be at some of the meetings but not this one. I'm bound to make a lash-up now even though I've been practising all week."

"Don't be daft," hissed Bernie the Boatman, glancing towards the corner where Brett stood talking to Robert. "He's a nice bloke so there's nothing to be scared of."

"Are you after a part then, Bernie?" Marlene asked, "You don't usually."

"Yep, I thought I'd give it a go this year and try for the gardener. After all I'm used to all this theatrical stuff having played Father Christmas at the Wonderland these past two years."

Marlene giggled. "Not quite the same though, is it? I mean, all you have to remember to say as Father Christmas is ho ho ho, the rest is adlibbed."

"True but then the gardener doesn't have much to say so I can handle that."

After the meeting several group members went to the Crown and Anchor, some to quench their thirst, others to steady their nerves. The auditions had gone well and Robert had promised to phone those who were to be offered parts the following morning.

There was a lot of excited chatter in the pub; several expressed their hopes and others their anguish over the fact that their auditions hadn't quite gone to plan.

Seeing Alina the actress standing alone, looking lost, while Brett and Robert sat in the corner discussing the auditions, Tess crossed over to speak to her.

"You look lonely."

Alina smiled. "Do I? Yes, I suppose I must do. I don't know anyone you see apart from Brett and Robert and they've both deserted me."

"Come on, let's sit down. I'm Tess by the way, Tess Dobson, and I'd like to hear a bit about you. You're an actress, I believe."

"Yes, but not a well-known one although I do have a fairly good part coming up and we start filming soon. It's a drama series but I can't tell you anything about it as we're sworn to secrecy."

"Fair enough."

"Have you lived in Pentrillick long, Tess?"

"Yes, all my life and I wouldn't want to live anywhere else."

"I can understand that, it's beautiful. The reason I ask is because when Brett bought the cottage the name of the village rang a bell. Wasn't there a robbery here a few years back? I vaguely remember reading about it. The name Pentrillick stuck in my mind you see because I thought it charming."

"Well remembered. Yes, there was and it made the television news too. It's Pentrillick House that was broken into and it happened while the owners, the Liddicott-Treens, were on holiday. Several items of value were stolen and sadly never retrieved."

"Pentrillick House, yes that was the name. I imagined it to be a gorgeous country estate," She giggled, "a bit like Mulberry Hall."

"I suppose it is. You must go and see it sometime. Get Brett to take you, it's well worth a visit."

"You mean it's open to the public?"

"Yes, all the year round."

"Wow! I'll do that then." Alina glanced across the bar and caught Brett's eye. To her delight he beckoned her over.

She smiled broadly. "I must go. Thanks for chatting to me, Tess. I really appreciate it."

"My pleasure."

When Hetty spotted Tess was momentarily on her own she dragged Lottie from her seat. "Quick, we need to speak to Tess."

After asking Tess if she knew anything of their mystery visitor they were surprised and disappointed to hear her say that she didn't although she was very interested. However, standing close by was Kitty who overheard what was said.

"Did I hear right?" Kitty asked, turning to face the three women, "that Lucy Lacey called at Primrose Cottage today?"

"Lucy Lacey, is that her name?" Hetty asked.

"Well, yes, if we're talking about the same person. Lucy is in her early seventies. She's slim, about five feet tall and a bit of a recluse."

"She certainly fits that description although I thought she looked older than that," said Lottie, "Do you know her then?" Hetty was eager to learn more.

"Vaguely. We were at primary school together although she's a few years older than me. She lives at Wood Cottage a small house on moorland not far from Pentrillick Woods. Her family have lived there for generations but since her parents both died she's been on her own."

"Did she ever marry?" Hetty asked.

"No, she didn't although I recall hearing she had a boyfriend many years ago but that would have been while she was away."

"Away?" Hetty queried.

"Yes, if I remember correctly she moved to Plymouth. I don't know why but I suppose it would have been to work. Anyway, she came home when her father died so her mother wouldn't be on her own, but she must have been close to retirement age by then anyway because it's got to be well over ten years ago. Her father worked at Pentrillick House in the grounds as did his father and grandfather before him. When Lucy's father retired the Liddicott-Treens gave him the cottage as a retirement present. Of course it wasn't Tristan who was head of the house back then because he was only a lad. It was his father. Nice man as I recall. Very kind-hearted."

"He must have been to have given away a cottage," spluttered Lottie.

"Well, the Laceys had worked on the estate for over a hundred years between them so I suppose he thought they'd earned it."

"Lucky Laceys," said Hetty.

Kitty laughed. "When we were kids we used to call her Lucky Lucy but that was because her mother sold white heather as did her grandmother and now it appears she does too."

"Perhaps that accounts for their luck as regards the cottage," reasoned Hetty, "the heather I mean."

"Probably," Kitty sighed, "Poor Lucy, I don't think she's ever had any real friends. Not when she was in Cornwall anyway but she always seemed happy enough. I haven't seen her for years as she's inclined to keep herself to herself."

"Without doubt, that'll be her then," stated Hetty, as she produced the sprig of white heather from her pocket. "I bought it to bring me luck at the auditions."

"Well let's hope it works," giggled Tess, amazed that any knowledge of Lucy Lacey had passed her by.

Kitty looked puzzled. "Yes, but I wonder why she didn't come to us. I know she didn't because I've been in all day."

"She might have called at our place," reflected Tess, "but if she did there would have been no-one at home, which is a shame because I felt I did badly tonight so could have done with a lucky charm."

Kitty glanced around. "Ah, there's Ginny so I'll ask if she called at their house."

"But surely Ginny would have been in the antique shop all day," reasoned Hetty.

"Damn, yes, of course. But Chloe might have been in. I'll go and ask her."

Lottie winked and nodded towards her sister. "Perhaps she has inside information and only calls on houses where the gullible live."

Hetty was indignant. "I am not gullible."

Kitty returned. "She did call at Tuzzy-Muzzy and Chloe bought a sprig of heather for the same reason as you, Het."

Hetty was just about to ask Kitty if Lucy had also read a broken biscuit for Chloe but then thought better of it. After all, the concept really was beyond crazy and she didn't want Tess and Kitty to agree with her sister that she was gullible.

The following morning, Hetty having slept badly, arose early just as it was getting light. She made herself a cup of tea and took it into the back garden where she sat beside the pond and watched the sun rise. Before long the garden was bathed in sunshine and it felt as though it was going to be a beautiful spring-like day. But after a while she began to feel chilly and returned indoors just as Lottie came down the stairs.

"You got up early, Het."

"I couldn't sleep. Silly I know but I'm a bag of nerves this morning."

Lottie laughed. "Why on earth are you getting all wound up by a part in a village play? Anyone would think you were hoping to join a West End show."

"I know, I know it's ridiculous but I've got a bee in my bonnet about playing the cook and dread being disappointed." Hetty paced the floor.

Lottie tutted. "Cup of coffee? It might help calm your nerves."

"Yes, please."

As Lottie switched on the kettle, the telephone rang in the hallway. Hetty jumped and her face turned white. "That's early. It's not even nine yet."

"Perhaps Robert is an early riser."

"Or it's a nuisance call." Hetty half hoped it was.

The phone continued to ring.

"Well go and answer it," Lottie urged, noting his sister was standing rigid.

Hetty cautiously picked up the receiver. It was Robert and she felt sure he must have heard her heart thumping. After greeting her briefly he offered her the part of Mrs Appleby the cook.

"I can't believe it," chuckled Hetty, as she put down the receiver and skipped into the kitchen, "I feel like a kid the night before Christmas. Robert sounded in a really good mood." Hetty picked up the sprig of white heather and kissed it, "And thank you, Lucy Lacey. I'll be forever in your debt."

"I'm pleased for you, Het. I really am."

"Thank you, it should be great fun. Robert said because they're short of men he's going to ask Vicar Sam if he'll play the part of the police sergeant because no-one auditioned for it. He asked me if I thought he could and would do it and I said yes."

"And very good he'd be too," agreed Lottie, handing a mug of coffee to her sister, "after all being a vicar he's used to an audience."

"Exactly. Chloe got the part she wanted too as the housekeeper and Bernie is to be the gardener. He didn't say who the other parts were going to because he's not phoned them all yet." Hetty grinned from ear to ear. "Apparently Brett was very impressed by the auditions so that's a feather in all our caps."

They walked into the sitting room and sat down at the table by the window.

"So will Brett be at the first rehearsal next week?" Lottie asked.

"No, because he and Alina are going back to London tomorrow."

"That was a quick visit then. They only arrived yesterday."

"Hmm, good point, so perhaps they came down because Brett wanted to have a say in the auditions."

"And who can blame him after all he doesn't want his name associated with a flop."

"I've just remembered someone else who has been offered and has accepted a part. Marlene, she's to be the hairstylist's wife."

"Really, so she's the one who does you in."

Hetty scowled. "Yes, I hadn't thought of that."

"And she's the leading lady. Good for her because I thought she was excellent when she auditioned for the part."

Hetty's frowned; her verbal response was little more than a grunt.

Chapter Five

"This weather is bonkers," chuntered Hetty, as she came in from the back garden and warmed her hands by the fire on St Patrick's Day. "I can't believe more snow is forecast this weekend and that we need to cover the tender plants again especially after yesterday when it was warm and spring-like. Poor birds, poor garden plants, they must be as disorientated as I feel."

"I assume it's cold out there already then," said Lottie, without looking up from her knitting.

"Cold, it's damn near freezing despite the sunshine. Roll on summer. We deserve a good one after what we've had to put up with this winter."

"Hmm, now that would be nice."

The next morning was bitterly cold again but the sun was shining and so the sisters were happy to go to church, especially Hetty who was keen to see if the vicar had agreed to join the cast of *Murder at Mulberry Hall*.

After the service, Vicar Sam shook hands with his parishioners outside the church porch. When it was the turn of the sisters, Hetty didn't mince her words. "I heard you were to be asked to play the part of the police sergeant," she blurted, "I do hope you've accepted."

A huge grin crossed the vicar's face. "How could I refuse? Robert was very persuasive and to be honest it'll make a pleasant change."

"Oh, that's brilliant. I think it's going to be a lot of fun and I can't wait for rehearsals to get underway tomorrow."

"It'll certainly be fun playing alongside Sid," laughed the vicar, "I can't imagine him being serious for one minute."

"Me neither."

"So what part is Sid playing?" Lottie asked.

Hetty chuckled. "The detective inspector."

"Oh dear, but then it is supposed to be a comedy."

"And you I hear are the cook, Hetty, who meets with an unfortunate end," teased the vicar. "I hope you're good at keeping very still and holding your breath."

"I can assure you I shall practise until the cows come home because I'm determined not to let the side down."

It was still bitterly cold as the sisters walked back to Primrose Cottage at a quick pace to prevent their toes and fingers from going numb. Once home, while Lottie made up the fire, Hetty boiled a kettle and poured the hot water onto the block of ice in the birdbath which stood in the front garden where it could be observed from the sitting room window.

"I was thinking about the Pentrillick House robbery while we were in church," said Lottie, when both were seated in the sitting room with mugs of coffee, warming their toes by the fire, "and I can't help but wonder if it was done by someone living locally. What do you think?"

"Highly unlikely because the goods would be worthless unless they were turned into cash. Professional thieves know where to dispose of stolen things and I think most folks around here are pretty law abiding. What makes you think it might have been locals?"

"I'm not sure. Probably because whoever it was knew the Liddicott-Treens were away and that they knew their way around the house."

"But anyone could have found out they were away and remember the alarm system was deactivated and they used explosives to blow open the secure door of the room where the goods were on display. Hardly the work of petty thieves."

Lottie looked downcast. "Hmm, I suppose you're right. I wish we'd been around when it happened though as I should like to know more but it's not much use taking an interest now as the scent will have long gone cold."

"Oh, I don't know. It wouldn't do any harm for us to make a few enquiries after all we're good at solving mysteries."

"Are we?"

"Yes, of course. Well, we do our best."

In the afternoon it snowed and once again Cornwall was a white world. Hetty, fearing the first rehearsal might be cancelled was fed up. But the following morning Kitty called round to visit the sisters with good news.

"I thought you'd like to know that tonight's rehearsal for the play will go ahead."

Hetty rubbed her hands gleefully as she escorted Kitty into the sitting room. "That's excellent news. I must admit I thought it might be called off when I saw it was snowing again this morning."

Kitty sat down. "Me too but it's melting at a furious rate now, thank goodness, and the lane is already quite dry."

"There's hope for my tomato seeds yet then because I noticed this morning that some have germinated. In fact I must remember to put them on the window sill so they can get some natural light."

"How many have come up?" Lottie asked.

"About half a dozen which is perfect because we don't really want more than that."

The following weekend the clocks went forward so it was quite dark when the sisters rose, determined to attend the Palm Sunday morning service at nine o'clock. When Lottie pulled back the sitting room curtains she glanced down at the seed tray containing the tomato seedlings and chuckled.

"Have you counted your tomatoes recently?" she called to Hetty who was in the kitchen.

"No, why? Don't tell me they've died."

"Far from it. There are forty three now."

"Forty three," repeated Hetty, as she entered the sitting room with two mugs of tea.

"Yes, and I think there are a few more peeping through."

"Just as well we both like tomatoes then."

Once outside they found there was a hint of spring in the air spoiled only by a cold wind.

"It's mornings such as this that make me glad to be alive," sang Hetty, as they walked down Long Lane, "before we know it there will be signs of life in the hedgerows, birds will be singing and the grass verges will be a blaze of colour."

"A lovely thought," Lottie agreed, "and thank goodness we're on the right side of winter now. Although having said that, I do like autumn."

"Hmm, me too. In fact all seasons have their merits and it's only when they go on for too long that they become tiresome."

"Yes, like this winter has."

When they left the church after Sung Eucharist, Hetty looked a little subdued and told Lottie she was concerned about Vicar Sam, for during the service he had repeatedly looked at his watch and seem distracted. Lottie agreed.

"Is everything okay, Sam?" Hetty gabbled, unable to hide her intrigue, "It's just you don't seem your usual bouncy self this morning."

Lottie nodded. "I agree and I do hope you're not coming down with something nasty. Especially now, just before Easter."

Vicar Sam smiled broadly. "Thank you for your concern, ladies, but I can assure you that I'm fine. It's just that, well…."

"…Co ee," called a singsong voice, "we're here."

All three turned and looked towards the church gate where a woman dressed in a chocolate brown funnel neck coat furiously waved and the man at her side smiled broadly.

Vicar Sam heaved a sigh of relief. "Thank goodness, you had me worried you're usually so punctual."

"Punctual is the operative word, well nearly," laughed the man, "We had a puncture you see on the way down."

Vicar Sam tutted and turned to the sisters. "Hetty, Lottie, please allow me to introduce you to my zany parents, Penelope and Michael."

Penelope squeezed Vicar Sam's hand, pecked his cheek and then turned to the sisters. "Pleased to meet you, ladies. I assume you are members of Sammy's congregation."

"Yes, we are," declared Hetty, "and it's nice to meet you too. Are you down for Easter?"

"Yes. We're down for a whole fortnight and we're really looking forward to it. I just hope the weather warms up a bit. It's been beastly cold of late."

"Especially the 'Beast from the East' as the press have called it," chortled Michael.

Sam tutted. "I've been quite worried, you know, because you were adamant you'd be here on time for the service and I wrote the sermon with you in mind."

"Sorry, Sammy," consoled Penelope, "but you can tell us the nature of your lecture later."

"Mother, my sermons are not lectures."

Penelope's face indicated she thought otherwise.

"Well, we did intend to be here in time for the service," insisted Michael, "but as I said we had a wretched puncture. I have to admit the traffic was quite heavy too despite our early start so we probably still wouldn't have made it. Sorry, son."

"Did you change the wheel yourself?" asked Lottie, who had recently read about the process on-line.

Michael nodded. "Yes, I used to be a mechanic before I retired so it was a piece of cake."

Hetty was inquisitive. "Have you come far?"

"Exeter," Michael answered, "so not too far at all."

"Still a two or three hour drive though." Lottie who, as a relatively new driver, considered that quite far enough.

"So will you be staying at the Vicarage?" Hetty asked, keen to know the facts.

"Absolutely," said Penelope, "it would be silly to stay anywhere else when Sammy has two spare bedrooms."

"Yes, of course, anyway we'd better be off. I'm sure you've lots to do if you've only just arrived." Hetty took her gloves from her handbag and put them on.

"And lots to talk about as well," Lottie added.

"Yes, we have," declared Penelope, "I want to tell Sammy about our new neighbours. I hope to see you ladies again soon."

"Likewise. Goodbye, Sam. See you at tomorrow's rehearsal. That's if you can make it."

"Oh, I'll be there without question."

"Rehearsal?" Penelope queried.

"Yes, I've been roped into the drama group's latest play. I'm a police sergeant."

"Oh, that I must see. When will it be performed?"

"In the summer sometime. I don't know when."

"The end of May," disclosed Hetty, "half term week."

"Ah, yes, Whit week," said the vicar.

"Well," chuckled Penelope, "I shall put it in my diary right now and make sure we pop back for it."

As she searched through her handbag for the diary the sisters said farewell and left the churchyard for the walk home.

"I wonder what it is about the new neighbours that Penelope feels they must tell Sam about," said Hetty as they walked back up Long Lane.

"You're so nosy, Het."

"I know but I can't help it. Anyway, if they're here for a fortnight I'm sure the opportunity will arise for me to find out."

Chapter Six

On Wednesday evening, Gideon Elms said goodbye to Debbie, his wife of forty years, and then left their home in St. Mary's Avenue for the short walk to the church for the weekly choir practice. Tucked beneath his arm was a box of assorted broken biscuits given to him by the vicar's mother who thought it would be nice for him to share them with the choir when they had tea and coffee after the practice.

Gideon and Debbie were relatively new to Pentrillick having moved to the village the previous October following Gideon's retirement from working as head groundsman at a public school. The couple had at first been a little apprehensive about making new friends in the autumn of their years but the church had made them feel welcome and both were very fond of Vicar Sam. Kitty Thomas had also become a good friend; she was the church organist and when she learned that Gideon could also play they had agreed to take it in turns to play at the services. Furthermore, Kitty, on learning of Gideon's erstwhile occupation, suggested should he be interested that there was a part-time vacancy at Pentrillick House for a gardener. And Gideon, keen to keep active, applied for and to his delight was awarded the job.

As Gideon approached the church he saw Hazel Mitchell who he recognised as a cook who worked at Pentrillick House, standing at the bus stop. He wished her a good evening and then climbed the steps and walked along the church's gravel path, his fingers crossed hoping that choir practice, the last before Easter, would go smoothly and quash all qualms he'd had a few weeks earlier when the new anthem he and Kitty wanted the choir to learn looked an impossible task.

As he stepped into the church and looked across the empty pews in the fading light of day, it appeared that he was the first to have arrived. However, as he closed the door and switched on the lights, he heard a noise coming from inside the vestry and saw a sudden flash of light.

"Is that you, Kitty?" Gideon called, as he removed his cap and walked towards the vestry where a long red curtain hung from its archway entrance. The noise stopped abruptly but no-one answered. Confused by the lack of response he pushed aside the heavy curtain and entered the area where the choir's cassocks and surplices hung from two rows of pegs alongside a tall cupboard. To his surprise no-one was there but an ancient chest containing old books and other items no longer in use was open and some of its contents were scattered across the floor. Gideon was puzzled. He scratched his head. Who had opened it and why? Filled with curiosity, he stepped forward to take a closer look and was further surprised when he saw a mobile phone lying on the floor. As he reached out to pick it up he was distracted by a faint sound in the main body of the church; a squeak similar to the noise made by the squeaky ball much loved by his dear old dog who had died shortly after his retirement. Gideon stood perfectly still and listened, but all was silent. And then suddenly he heard it again, another squeak. Simultaneously, the phone on the floor rang and its screen flashed. From the corner of his eye, Gideon saw the heavy curtain move; a gloved hand appeared and slowly pulled aside the dark red fabric. In a flash a brilliant light shone into his eyes. Gideon shrieked in alarm. Blinded by the brightness he dropped the box of biscuits and with arms across his face backed away from the light. Desperate to know who held the torch, he attempted to open his eyes and as he blinked he caught a whiff of scent or aftershave. And then everything went black as something hard and heavy crashed down upon his head.

"Listen, there's another one." Hetty put aside the book she was reading and sat up straight. "Did you hear that, Lottie? The siren I mean. That's the third one I've heard in the last five minutes and they all appear to be down in the village."

Lottie glanced up from her knitting. "Yes, I did but I daresay it's nothing to get excited about and if it is we'll no doubt hear when we next go out."

"When we next go out!" Hetty stood up. "That's all very well but I want to find out now." She walked towards the door: "Something must be visible from upstairs so I'm going to take a peep from my bedroom window."

Lottie chuckled to herself as her sister ran noisily up the stairs and across the floor of her room. However, her curiosity was also raised when she heard her sister scream.

"Goodness me, come up here and see this, Lottie. There are lots of blue lights flashing along the main street."

Lottie put down her knitting and joined her sister.

"Whereabouts do you think that is?" Lottie asked, as they both hung their heads from the open window, "It's tricky to make it out when it's nearly dark."

"Somewhere near the church and Sea View Cottage, I reckon. Look you can just make out the outline of the church tower in the street lights."

"You're right. Oh dear, there must have been an accident of some sort."

"Let's go down to the pub and see if we can find out what's going on."

Lottie looked reluctant. "But if there's been a nasty accident I don't think I want to know."

"But it might not be an accident. It might be a robbery of some sort. Remember, you said you'd like to be able to solve the mystery of the Liddicott-Treens' burglary at Pentrillick House. Well, now's your chance, There might be a connection."

"And pigs might fly," scoffed Lottie.

Hetty closed the window. "You don't want to come with me then?"

"I didn't say that."

"Good, let's get our shoes on."

When they reached the bottom of Long Lane they cast their eyes along the main street but because of a bend it was not possible to see as far as the emergency vehicles.

"Shall we walk a little way along?" Hetty took a few steps towards the bend.

"No." Lottie was adamant. "I don't want to see anything horrible, Het. It'd be insensitive, not to mention very bad manners."

Hetty's shoulders slumped. "Yes, you're right. I must try and curb my inquisitive nature. Anyway, hopefully someone in the pub will know what's going on."

Inside the Crown and Anchor tongues wagged and voices were raised as all tried to establish the reason for the emergency vehicles. After buying drinks, the sisters sat down and eagerly listened to the excited chatter.

"There's an ambulance as well as the cop cars," announced someone with whom Hetty and Lottie were not acquainted, "I saw them on my way here and there were lights on in the church too."

"Well that would be because it's choir practice night," said Bernie the Boatman. "My wife was a bundle of nerves when she went off tonight. She's worried you see that she'll get the harmony wrong in the piece they're doing for Easter. Gideon told 'em they had to get it right tonight. Poor Veronica."

"She'll be alright," remarked Sid, "she's got a smashing voice."

"Yes, I know that but she's not used to singing the harmony."

As he spoke, a man about five foot six in height with rugged features and nicotine stained fingers entered the pub. He wore a shabby leather jerkin over the top of a dark green fleece top and a knitted woollen hat which he removed as he approached the bar.

"Rum do back there," he croaked, as he lay down his hat on a stool, "I hope the poor sod's not dead."

He sat down and ordered a pint of cider while he tried to catch his breath. The bar went quiet and everyone moved a little closer to hear what he had to say.

"Are you talking about whatever's going on up the road, Pickle?" Bernie asked.

He nodded. "Yes, some poor bloke's been attacked."

"Ah, so that's what all the commotion up the road's about?" said Marlene, the drama group's leading lady, as she entered the pub with her husband, Gary.

"So he's Pickle," whispered Hetty behind her hand, "We've seen him on several occasions, haven't we, Lottie?"

"Yes, and little did we realise he's Pentrillick's notorious poacher."

"Any idea who it is? The bloke who was attacked, I mean." Ashley, the landlord asked.

Pickle took a sip of his drink. "According to some bystanders it's that chap Gideon who plays the organ and he was attacked in the church. It was poor old Kitty Thomas who found him."

Everyone gasped.

The colour drained from Hetty's face. "Poor Kitty. Poor Gideon."

"Gideon," shouted Marlene, as she removed her faux fur jacket and draped it over a stool, "What Gideon our next door neighbour?"

"Well, there's only one Gideon as I know of in the village," said Pickle. "Does your neighbour play the organ in the church?"

Marlene nodded. "Yes."

"That'll be him then."

"Oh dear, he's a miserable sod but I wish him no harm." Marlene looked genuinely upset.

"Are you alright, Het, because you look awful?" Lottie asked.

Hetty didn't speak but from her handbag she took the sprig of white heather.

Lottie gasped. "You're thinking about what Lucy said."

Hetty nodded.

Marlene sat down heavily on a stool. "Why would anyone attack Gideon and in the church of all places? Is nothing sacred anymore?"

"Don't look like it," agreed Bernie.

The door opened and Luke Burleigh and his wife Natalie who lived in a cottage along the main street walked in.

"In case you're wondering," said Luke, noting that everyone in the pub seemed to be in a joint conversation, "it looks as though Gideon's going to be alright. He's gained consciousness and has been taken off to hospital."

"You sure?" Ashley asked.

Luke nodded. "Yes, we've just been up to Meadowsweet to fetch Kitty's husband, Tommy, because she was asking for him. Don't know whether or not you know but it was Kitty who found Gideon and needless to say she's pretty upset."

"Any idea what happened?" Pickle asked.

"Not for sure but word has it he might have disturbed a burglar because one of the choir boys said the brass candlesticks on the altar have gone missing."

Hetty looked at the sprig of white heather and laid it on the palm of her hand. *"I see yellow tulips in a shaft of sunlight. I see a lady cooking and she will get hurt. Other people will get hurt. Some will be deceitful. Things will go missing. Nothing will make sense. But you dear lady shall be unhurt for the lucky heather will protect you and your family.*" She looked at Lottie, "Gideon is hurt and the candlesticks are missing."

Lottie shuddered. "Yes, I must admit that is a little uncanny."

"Very uncanny." Hetty sat in a daze.

"But it must be a coincidence." Lottie was determined not to be beguiled.

Hetty didn't answer.

"It's a little unnerving as well," Lottie persisted, "The attack, I mean, not Lucy's um…er…reading. I mean, who on earth could do such a thing?"

Hetty just sat quietly her eyes transfixed on the heather.

"I suppose we could always try and find out, Het." Lottie hoped the suggestion would jolt her sister out of the trance.

The dazed look on Hetty's face began to fade and her mouth opened into a smile. "But how on earth do you propose we do that, Lottie? We haven't been near the church so have no more to go on than anyone else in this pub."

"Well I suppose we could question Gideon when he comes out of hospital…"

"…Oh Lottie, don't be silly. He won't be able to tell us anything that he'll not have told the police."

"It's not like you to be negative, Het."

"I'm not being negative. Am I?"

"Yes you are."

"Humph, well that won't do." Hetty picked up her glass and took a large gulp of wine. "Okay, we'll try and find out who did it and perhaps at the same time we'll see if we can shed some light on the theft at Pentrillick House. After all you said you'd like to know more about it and if I'm honest, so should I."

Lottie smiled. "That's the spirit."

"But I must admit I don't hold out much hope. What's more it's nearly Easter and the family will be here tomorrow so we won't have much time to go probing into crimes past or present."

"There's no rush, Hetty. It can be our summer project along with the play of course."

Hetty thought again of Lucy's prediction. She shuddered and then dropped the sprig of heather back into her handbag.

Chapter Seven

The following day was Maundy Thursday and across the country schools broke up for the Easter holiday. In a quiet Northamptonshire village, after a bus had dropped off the school children, the Burton family put the last of their luggage into the boot of their car and were ready to leave their home for the drive to Cornwall.

"Say goodbye to the peace and quiet," laughed Lottie, several hours later when they heard the family car pull up on the driveway.

"I'm actually looking forward to a bit of noise and disruption," admitted Hetty, waving to the family from the sitting room window. "Remember how quiet it was when Zac went home after spending the school holiday with us last summer. It took us both quite a while to get used to the silence."

"I remember it well but there was only one of him and he doesn't have a high-pitched voice like the girls nor does he get overexcited."

"Perhaps they'll have quietened down a bit now they're fifteen." Hetty was hopeful.

"I very much doubt it because in my opinion the older they get the more racket they make. Until they get to be about twenty that is, after that they seem to settle down."

"Are you speaking from experience?"

Lottie laughed. "Yes, I've a very good memory of what you were like."

"Cheeky."

Albert barked sensing strangers were approaching the house. Hetty picked him up while Lottie opened the door. Two teenage girls tumbled in.

"There's Albert," screamed Vicki. The dog leapt from Hetty's arms on hearing his name with tail wagging nineteen to the dozen, "bagsy I hold the lead first when we take him for a walk."

"That's not fair, you always get in first," snapped her twin sister, Kate, "you wouldn't have even remembered him if I hadn't mentioned him in the car."

Hetty winked at Lottie. "I see what you mean."

"Stop arguing, girls, and say hello to your grandmother and great aunt," ordered Bill, as he hugged the two ladies in turn. The girls did as they were asked.

"Good journey?" Lottie asked.

"So, so," said Sandra, "we've passed through quite a few showers but the roads weren't too busy."

"Probably because Easter's early this year." Lottie closed the door as they took off their coats.

"What about your luggage?" Hetty asked, noting they were all emptyhanded, "If I were you I would get it in while it's fine."

"Good idea," agreed Bill, "Give us a hand, please, Zac."

"Can we explore?" Kate eagerly asked, as she hopped from foot to foot.

"Yes, off you go," sighed Lottie, "You're both in the twin room in the loft conversion next to your mum and dad."

Kate raced up the stairs closely followed by Vicki and an over excited Albert.

"Go quietly," shouted Sandra, "you're not at home now."

"I see one of the twins has had her hair cut," remarked Hetty, as the girls disappeared round the corner at the top of the stairs.

"Yes, Vicki has," said Sandra, "she got it cut last week because she was fed up with having long hair. I think it looks rather nice."

Hetty smiled. "I couldn't agree more and now for the first time in years I'll actually be able to tell them apart."

"Yes, I have to agree," Sandra confessed, "Having identical twin daughters can be hard work at times."

Bill and Zac brought in the luggage and laid it in the hallway; amongst the bags and suitcases was a huge bunch of yellow tulips. Sandra picked it up. "These are for you ladies. I spotted them at a service station and thought how bright and cheerful they looked."

Lottie took them from her daughter-in-law. "Thank you, Sandra, they're beautiful." She nudged her sister who appeared too shocked to speak. "Yes, yes, they are," mumbled Hetty, "Thank you, dear. I'll find a vase for them."

More squeals followed from upstairs.

Lottie nodded to Hetty. "I'll make a pot of tea, it looks like Sandra could do with a cup."

Hetty gazed at the yellow tulips. "She's not the only one."

In the evening, after the family had settled in they all went down to the Crown and Anchor for a meal where many were debating the whys and wherefores of the attack on Gideon Elms the previous day.

"Have the police found the weapon that poor old Gideon was hit with?" Bill heard someone ask as he waited at the bar to order their food.

"No," came the reply, "but word has it that it might have been a candlestick because the pair on the altar are both missing."

Bill reported his hearing to the family.

"A candlestick," Lottie repeated, "that seems very likely because they're quite a weight and we've heard whatever was used was a blunt and heavy instrument."

"Or maybe they're just missing because they were stolen," reasoned Kate, who was getting more and more intrigued by the mystery, "they'd be worth a fortune if they're real gold."

"I think they're more likely to be real brass," chuckled Bill.

"Was anything else taken?" Sandra asked, "other than the candlesticks, that is."

"Not that we're aware of," conceded Lottie, "but it's early days yet and no doubt we'll get a lot more information once it gets into the right hands."

"Namely Tess," chuckled Hetty, looking towards the bar where the lady in question was pouring drinks.

"Tess?" repeated Sandra.

"Yes, if you want to find out the latest news then you need look no further than Tess," Lottie declared.

"So, she's the local gossip," said Bill, "every village has one."

Hetty frowned. "Well I suppose so but she's much too nice a person to be labelled thus."

While the family were eating their meals in the bar, Brett and Alina who had arrived back the previous day to spend Easter in the village walked into the pub. Later in the Ladies, Hetty encountered Alina by the washbasins where she was waylaid by Marlene, the play's leading lady.

"Have you and Brett been questioned by the police about the attack on Gideon?" Marlene asked Alina. "I just wondered because it's possible you might have seen or heard something with Sea View Cottage being nearly opposite the church." Marlene turned off the tap and held her hands beneath the drier.

"Yes, we have but we didn't hear or see anything. Brett was in the bath at that time and I was watching television. It would have been nearly dark anyway by half seven, wouldn't it?"

"Hmm, probably. I get a bit muddled about times when the clocks have just been altered."

"Me too. Anyway, the first we knew of it was when the sirens stopped outside and we saw flashing blue lights through the curtains."

Hetty with ears flapping and keen to learn anything she could about the case, eavesdropped on the conversation while applying fresh lipstick and to make sure she didn't miss anything she also brushed her hair.

"How about you?" Alina asked, as she took a bottle of expensive looking perfume from her handbag and sprayed some on her wrists, "Have you been questioned by the police?"

"Oh yes because we live next door to Gideon and Debbie." She sniffed the air. "Hmm, that reminds me of a rose my granny had in her garden when I were a kid." Alina's eyebrows twitched. "Yes, anyway as I was saying, me and hubby have both been questioned but we have good alibis in each other. Not that I expect we'll be suspects. I mean, if we wanted to hurt Gideon why would we follow him to the church when he only lives next door?"

Alina shrugged her shoulders. "Don't know."

"Anyway, as I said we're each other's alibis. Gary was watching football or it might have been rugby. It was sport anyway and I was curled up in the armchair learning my words as I'm determined to be a credit to your Brett."

Alina smiled falsely. She was used to people and women in particular, being friendly towards her with the sole intent of getting into Brett's good books.

"Just a minute, you were in here last night," blurted Hetty without thinking as Marlene's claim sank in.

Marlene scowled. "Yes," she hissed, "we were later on when the football or whatever finished but that was sometime after Gideon was attacked."

Alina looked surprised.

"Yes, yes, of course, sorry." Hetty wished the floor would open up and swallow her.

On Good Friday morning, Lottie was busy in the kitchen making hot crossed buns.

"I don't know why you're bothering, Lottie," scoffed Hetty, "It seems silly to go to so much trouble for something readily available in the shops."

Bill tutted. "Oh no, I must disagree with you there. Shop-bought buns could never be as good as Mother's. Can't beat homemade."

"Well, we shall see. The proof is in the pudding and all that."

After Lottie had kneaded the spicy dough packed with dried fruit she returned it to the mixing bowl and covered it with clingfilm. She then carried the bowl outside and placed it in the lean-to greenhouse on the side of the garage. When she returned she pointed to Hetty's tomato seedlings on the sitting room window sill.

"It's lovely and warm in the greenhouse, Het. I reckon you could safely put your tomatoes and chillies out there and it'd stop the tomatoes getting even more leggy."

"I might do that because I can always bring them indoors at night if it looks like being cold."

"Looks to me like you need to prick the tomatoes out," laughed Bill, "you've quite a forest there."

"Yes, alright don't nag like your mother. I know I sowed too many but they'll not go to waste and I'll prick them out tomorrow."

"I'll do it for you now, if you like," proposed Sandra, "I like to make myself useful."

"Oh bless you, I'd really appreciate that because it's not a job I enjoy. The chillies are okay for a while because there are only six of them. Come with me and I'll show you where the pots and compost are."

At lunchtime, Bill popped down to the Crown and Anchor to have a pint with Bernie the Boatman with whom he had made friends two summers before.

"Many in there?" Sandra asked when he returned.

"Quite a few but then it is Easter."

"Try this on, Bill," said Lottie, throwing him the sweater she had finally finished knitting.

Bill caught it. "Will do. Something smells nice."

Lottie stood up. "It's the hot crossed buns and I need to take them out of the oven."

"Anyone in the pub you knew apart from Bernie?" Sandra asked as Lottie left the room.

"There were a few familiar faces and several people were talking about the attack on the organist again." Bill removed his jacket and pulled the sweater over his head.

"Hardly surprising," reasoned Sandra, "crime's not an everyday occurrence, especially in villages."

Bill looked at Hetty. "Are you and Mum trying to find out who did it, Auntie Het? The attack on the organist, I mean. Because surely it's right up your street."

Hetty laid down her script and looked over the top of her reading glasses. "Do I detect a hint of sarcasm in your voice, young man?"

"My dear, Auntie Hetty, whatever gives you that idea?"

"Cheeky boy," Hetty picked up her script, "The sweater looks very nice by the way. Your mother is a clever old stick."

"Thank you. I think I'll keep it on as it looks none too warm out."

"Very wise and in answer to your question, yes we are and it was your mother's idea; so we're currently keen to solve both mysteries. One, who stole certain items from Pentrillick House a few years back when the Liddicott-Treens were on holiday, and two, who brutally attacked our church organist last week?"

"And three," said Lottie, as she entered the sitting room, "who knocked the poor old heron in the pond? I've just noticed from the kitchen window that he's floating on the surface."

"That's an easy one to solve," giggled Kate, "It was Vicki. She stood him in the water to see how deep it was but he toppled over and then she couldn't reach him."

Chapter Eight

On Saturday morning, Penelope Prendergast left the Vicarage clutching two large baskets full to the brim with flowers and greenery. As she neared the village shop, she paused and then went inside enticed by the notion of a bag of mint humbugs. To her surprise the shop was busy. She selected the sweets she desired and then waited patiently in the queue to pay for her purchase.

"Hmm, those flowers smell divine," said Tess, also in the queue, "I love the scent of lilies. In fact I think they're my favourite flowers."

"So do I," agreed Penelope, "and these are special. They're for the church. The altar in fact. I asked Sammy weeks ago when I knew we'd be here for Easter if I could do them this Sunday. I love flower arranging, you see. It's my hobby."

"Sammy?" Tess was clearly puzzled.

"Vicar Sam," advised Kitty as she joined the queue, "this lady is his mother."

"Oh, I see. Pleased to meet you. I'm Tess Dobson."

"Penelope Prendergast," stated the vicar's mother, offering her hand as she placed one of the baskets on the floor.

After paying for her humbugs, Penelope left the shop and walked the short distance to the church. Once through the lichgate she quietly sang her favourite hymn and walked along the gravel path bordered on either side by banks of grass where daffodils bloomed amongst very old gravestones, many covered in lichen, and the final resting place of Pentrillick's long dead residents.

As she approached the solid wooden door, she took a large key from one of the baskets and inserted it into the lock. Usually the church was left unlocked during the day so that visitors might view the interior but since the attack on Gideon Elms the Parochial Church Council decided they must be more security conscious. After turning the key, Penelope carefully pushed open the door and stepped inside. She shivered. The building struck cold and eerie when devoid of human presence and the sunlight shining through the mullioned windows cast strange shadows across the cold stone floor. To ensure that she did not feel quite so alone, she left the door slightly ajar hopeful that the sound of passing traffic outside would provide a little comfort.

There were no flowers on the altar for the arrangement from the previous Sunday had been removed for the Good Friday services and in place of the missing candlesticks a similar pair which normally stood in the window behind the choir stalls now had pride of place on either end of the altar cloth.

Penelope filled the two brass vases with water from the tap in the belfry and then carefully and artistically arranged the flowers to her satisfaction, singing as she did so in a clear contralto voice. Feeling pleased with her effort, she stood back to admire her handiwork; all was well except for one of the lilies which needed to be turned slightly to the left. As she stepped forwards to adjust the flower she felt a sudden chill and sensed that she was being watched. Knowing what had happened to the organist she froze to the spot, afraid to turn around for fear of who or what she might see. Her mouth felt dry, her hands became clammy and she was conscious of her heart beating faster and much louder than usual. Desperate to know if her inkling was founded, she turned her head slowly just in time to glimpse movement by the door, and then it was gone. Feeling a sudden rush of bravery, Penelope picked up one of the replacement candlesticks and ran down the aisle and out of the door. But in the churchyard there was no sign of life other than a jackdaw resting on a nearby gravestone.

"I hope you'll all come to church with Auntie Hetty and me tomorrow," urged Lottie, on Saturday afternoon when the family returned from a trip out sightseeing, "After all it is Easter Sunday and it'd be nice to go as a family."

"I agree," said Bill, as he dropped his car keys into a pot on the mantelpiece, "I must admit I do like singing the old hymns so I hope there aren't too many I'm not familiar with."

Sandra smiled. "Well if there are I'm sure you'll soon get the hang of them after all you're quite musical."

"Yes, but the trouble is we'll most likely be on the last verse when that happens."

"Will we be getting Easter eggs tomorrow?" Kate asked in anticipation.

"No," said Sandra, firmly, "you're too old now and you eat too many sweets already."

Lottie was touched by the disappointed look on her granddaughter's face. "Don't worry, Kate, I'm going to make a big chocolate cake iced with real chocolate so you'll not be deprived."

Vicki looked puzzled. "This service tomorrow: will this be in the same church where the poor bloke you told us about was bashed on the head?"

Lottie tutted. "Yes, Pentrillick only has the one church: it's called St. Marys, and as for the poor man who was brutally attacked the other day, your aunt and I will be eager to hear how he's getting along. Poor Gideon."

Hetty nodded. "Quite right, but there is another church in the village although most people refer to it as the chapel. It's Methodist, you see."

"Wesleyan," corrected Lottie.

"Well, whatever it's still a chapel."

"Anyway you can count me in for a trip to the church," said Zac, "because it'll be great to see Sam again."

Vicki frowned. "Who's Sam?"

"The vicar," answered Lottie, "but he's usually referred to as Vicar Sam."

"Unless you're his mother," laughed Hetty. "She calls him Sammy."

Zac gasped. "She doesn't."

"She does," retorted Hetty, "and I get the impression he doesn't really like it."

"You're dead right," Zac agreed, "I remember someone calling him Sammy last summer and he went nuts."

"Ah, but mothers can get away with murder," said Lottie.

"Very true," agreed Bill.

Chapter Nine

On Easter Sunday morning the whole family left Primrose Cottage and walked down Long Lane into the village to the sound of the church bells ringing to entice villagers to join the worshippers. On the way they met Luke Burleigh out for a run. He nodded as he passed by.

"Does that bloke live near you because I've seen him running by several times?" Kate asked.

"He used to," replied Hetty, "but he and his wife live along the main street now."

"Rather him than me," chuntered Bill, glancing back at Luke, "Running, that is and up-hill too. He must be a health fanatic to be out this early in the morning."

"But it's nearly nine o'clock," laughed Sandra, "so hardly the crack of dawn."

"Actually, he's training for the London Marathon," Hetty revealed, "and he'll be raising money for charity."

Bill laughed. "Okay, I'll let him off then but I still think it's too early to be out running, especially on a Sunday and a cold Sunday to boot."

"He won't be cold if he's running," reasoned Lottie, "far from it."

Along the main road outside the church, cars were parked nose to tail leaving very little room for any late arrivals and near to the church gates the family passed visitors to Pentrillick who were reading of village events on the notice board.

Inside, Hetty and Lottie went to their usual pew. Zac sat with them but Bill, Sandra and the girls sat in front. No sooner were the girls seated than both had their phones out and were scrolling down the screens. Lottie tutted but decided it was not her place to reprimand her granddaughters. Besides, they were doing no harm.

At nine o'clock, the vicar and the choir left the vestry and processed down the aisle; the congregation stood to sing the first hymn and Sandra told the girls to put away their phones. They obeyed and half-heartedly attempted to sing but the words and tune were unfamiliar and so they opted to mime instead. Bill, however, made up for the lack of volume coming from the mouths of his daughters and sang with gusto.

At the end of the hymn they all sat and Vicar Sam addressed the congregation. Noticing him for the first time caused Vicki to gasp. "Who's he?" she whispered.

Sandra scowled. "Shush."

"Obviously the vicar, you numpty," whispered Kate, "Vicar Sam or whatever he's called. Surely you can tell that by his dog collar."

"Well yes I can but whatever he's drop-dead gorgeous…."

Vicki was forced to cease her chat when she received a sharp poke on the shoulder from her grandmother. After that the girls were both silent and during the sermon a little later, Sandra was surprised to see that her daughters appeared to hang on to every word spoken by the vicar.

After the service, Penelope Prendergast, the vicar's mother, greeted Hetty and Lottie. "Hello, ladies, lovely to see you again."

"Likewise," said Hetty, "and are you enjoying your stay?"

"Very much, thank you. Rum do about the organist chappie though."

"Gideon, yes," tutted Lottie, "I do hope they catch the person responsible but it seems the police have very little to go on."

"So I understand. Just as well you have a spare in Kitty. Organist that is."

"Actually Kitty has been playing for years but she was happy to share the duty with Gideon when he moved to the village and the two get on very well." Lottie stepped aside to let people pass by.

"Right, now, ladies, I know it's a bit of a silly question," said Penelope, biting her bottom lip, "but do you like biscuits?"

The sisters both laughed and then said they did.

"Would you like some then? They're assorted but broken."

"Oh, well, yes, that would be nice especially as the family are down for Easter," said Lottie.

"Good, I'll go and get some from the car. I'll be back in a jiffy."

"A whole box of broken biscuits," whispered Hetty, as Penelope left the church, "I dread to think what Lucy Lacey would say when confronted with that."

Lottie laughed. "Yes, I should imagine they'd put her in a right tiswas."

"Where are the family?" Hetty suddenly asked realising she was unable to see any of them.

"The girls are outside and Zac's gone to see Emma because he's been invited to lunch with her family. Bill and Sandra are over there chatting to Kitty." Lottie pointed to where they stood beside the font part hidden by a pillar.

"Here we are," gushed Penelope as she returned with a box, "I guarantee you'll like them as they're really delicious."

"But don't you want them?" Lottie asked.

"My dear, we have biscuits coming out of our ears. It's our new neighbours, you see. They've moved into the big house next door and they own a biscuit factory at which inevitably there are breakages every day. They're lovely people and when we first met them they kindly asked if we'd like some of the broken biscuits. We said yes and they've been giving us boxes ever since. We've both put on several pounds trying to get through them but in the end we started to stockpile them hoping to distribute them amongst Sammy's parishioners, as I'm doing now."

"I see, well that's very kind, thank you." Lottie took the box from Penelope. "I can assure you they'll not go to waste."

"Did you give some to Gideon?" Hetty asked on impulse, "It's just that I recall he had a box of broken biscuits with him on the night he was attacked."

"Yes, I did. He called round at the Vicarage the day after we arrived so I gave him a box then. He said he would share them with choir members after the next practice because he was confident they would have perfected the anthem he and Kitty had given them to learn."

"And it looks like he was right," smiled Lottie, "I thought the anthem was superb."

"Yes, just a pity poor Gideon wasn't able to hear it," sighed Hetty.

When they returned home from church, Lottie began to make preparations for the Sunday roast.

"Would there be any objections to me popping down the pub for a pint before dinner?" Bill asked.

"That's a good idea," agreed Sandra, "and I'll go with you. We'll take the girls too as I'm sure your mum and Auntie Het would appreciate a few minutes' peace."

Shortly after they left it began to rain. Hetty groaned. "It looks like it's going to be wet now for the rest of the day."

Lottie, took the parboiled potatoes from the hotplate. "That'll be quite nice because we can all stay indoors and watch a film or play Scrabble. Meanwhile, once these spuds are in the oven I must ice the chocolate cake or I'll have two irate teenager girls to contend with."

"And while you're doing that I'll make use of the quiet and attempt to learn my lines for the play."

Easter Monday began cold and dull after the rain the previous day but it brightened in the afternoon and encouraged people to get out and about despite the bitterly cold north wind. Pentrillick House was the destination of several hundred who wandered the grounds, shopped in the garden centre, toured the grand house and visited the lakeside café.

Inside the kitchen of Pentrillick House, Mrs Hazel Mitchell, a lady of fifty three summers, a widow and the family's part-time cook, was cosy and warm as she peeled apples to make a pie for the family's evening meal. However, her concentration wasn't for the job in hand, her thoughts were focused on the evening Gideon Elms had been attacked in the church. The reason for her concern was because when it happened she had been standing at the bus stop waiting to catch a bus into Helston where she was going to meet her friend, Andrew. She recalled seeing Gideon go into the church shortly after she had arrived at the bus stop and he called hello to her as he went through the church gates. A few minutes later, just as the bus arrived, she saw someone run from the church in an obvious state of distress. The person stopped, looked at Mrs Mitchell and their eyes momentarily met as she boarded the bus. She did not see where the person went as her attention was focussed on the driver who she was informing of her destination. When she sat down on the bus she glanced from the window hoping to catch a glimpse of the person she had seen, but it was almost dark and she saw little other than her own reflection in the glass. She thought no more about the incident until the next day when she heard about the attack on poor Gideon in the vestry. Hence, Hazel's dilemma; she felt that she ought to tell the police what she had seen although she doubted, if confronted with a line of possible suspects that she would be able to identify the person in question. The problem was Andrew. Neither of her two grown-up children liked him. They said he was a playboy who was only after the substantial amount of money she had obtained after the demise of their father, her husband. The house she lived in was bought and paid for and a large pay-out from an insurance policy meant she was comfortably off. In fact she didn't need to work at all but she'd taken the part-time job at Pentrillick House, when offered, because she loved cooking and wanted to get out and about and meet people.

Hazel laughed as she dropped the apple peel into a bowl ready to dispose of in the compost bin. The only reason she had taken the bus into Helston that night rather than her car was because Andrew lived quite near to her son and so she didn't want to park anywhere in that vicinity in case he spotted her car because she had told her children that she was no longer seeing Andrew. She knew it was a lie but she considered it to be just a little white lie. After all, she wasn't a fool and had no intention of letting Andrew get his hands on any of the money which she considered to be her children's inheritance. Anyway, he appeared to have plenty of money of his own although she did wonder where he got it from and on the few occasions she had mentioned it his response was very guarded; for that reason she often felt a little guilty and even wondered if her children might be right in their judgement.

From the refrigerator, Hazel took the pastry she had made earlier, rolled it out and placed it over the apples she had spiced with cinnamon. When the pie was ready she placed it in the oven, and took out a tray of ginger biscuits she'd made earlier for Jeremy, the Liddicott-Treen's fourteen year old son of whom she was very fond. She then washed down the old pine table where she'd worked and put the dirty dishes in the dish-washer.

Due to the heat from the Aga and the sun streaming in through one of the two windows, it was warm in the kitchen and so Hazel wasn't at all surprised when she caught sight of herself in the mirror to see that her cheeks were bright pink. Eager to cool down she walked towards an open window to lean out and get a breath of fresh air. But as she approached the window she sensed that someone was standing outside watching her. Slowly a gloved hand pulled the curtain aside. Hazel gasped, turned and ran towards the door eager to get out of the kitchen and into the hallway. In her haste she stumbled and knocked from the table the ginger biscuits which broke as they hit the flagstone floor. She attempted to scream but the noise from her mouth was little more than a squeak and as she reached for the door knob two shots were fired and her world went blank.

There was no drama group meeting on Easter Monday and so in the evening the family walked down to the Crown and Anchor for a drink. The pub was busy when they arrived and the chatter amongst the clientele seemed livelier than usual. Before she sat down Hetty popped to the Ladies to adjust an undergarment which she felt had come undone.

"What's with all the excitement?" Bill asked Bernie the Boatman, who sat on a stool at the bar talking to Vince from the garage, as he went to order drinks.

"Haven't you heard?" Bernie tutted and shook his head. "Poor old Hazel Mitchell was shot while she was at work in the kitchen of Pentrillick House this afternoon."

Bill's jaw dropped. "Shot! But that's terrible. Not that I know Hazel Mitchell. But is she alright? I mean, she obviously isn't but she is alive I hope."

"Yes, she is just about from what I've heard but it's not looking good."

Bill took his wallet from the pocket of his jeans. "So who is she?"

"She's the Liddicott-Treen's cook. Nice woman. Widowed a couple of years ago and I wouldn't have thought she was the sort of person to have had any enemies." Bernie took a sip of his beer, "I don't know what the world's coming to. First Gideon's attacked in the church of all places and now this."

"Who's next?" asked Ashley, the landlord from behind the bar.

Bill raised his hand and ordered drinks for the family. "Can I get you a drink, Bernie?"

"That's very kind but no. I'd better get going after this and tell Veronica what's happened. She liked Hazel you see. They were at school together."

"Oh dear, she's in for a bit of a shock then."

"She is and she's in the church choir too so knows Gideon as well."

When the drinks were ready Bill put them on a tray. "Well tell her we send our regards."

"Will do."

Bill picked up the tray and carried it to the table where the family sat.

"You'll never guess what," he said, as he handed out the glasses.

"Hazel Mitchell's been shot," blurted Lottie, clearly shaken, "we've just heard."

"Oh," Bill sounded disappointed.

"I told them," confessed Emma, who sat beside Zac. "It only happened a couple of hours ago and so everyone who was at Pentrillick House today is still there and no-one is allowed to leave until they've been questioned by the police. We were told about it by Mum who's up there with her sister, my Auntie May. She rang Dad a while back and said not to expect them home for a while."

"Wow, never a dull moment in this village." Bill sat down. "Where's Auntie Het?"

"In the Ladies." None of the family noticed the anxious look on Lottie's face and the fact she drummed her fingers on the table in an agitated manner.

"A few moments later Hetty returned. "Everything alright?" she asked as she removed her jacket and placed it on the back of a chair.

"We were just saying about the attempted murder at Pentrillick House," blurted Bill. He took a sip of his beer.

"Attempted murder?"

Lottie reached up and squeezed her sister's hand. "Yes, Het. It's Hazel Mitchell, the Liddicott-Treen's cook. She's been shot."

Hetty attempted to speak but no words came from her mouth. Voices all around her became muffled and her vision blurred. As a whooshing sound in her head grew louder and louder, she attempted to grab the back of a chair but missed as she fainted.

Several people panicked, one or two screamed, dreading the fact that Hetty might be victim number three but when she came round she assured everyone gathered around that she was not ill or hurt. Bill and Sandra each took one of her arms and helped her to a seat.

"It was the shock of hearing about Hazel," Hetty whispered, aware that her voice lacked its usual timbre, "I didn't know her but the fact she's a cook unnerved me."

"Ah, I expect it was because of the play," reasoned Bernie, sympathetically, "that was the first thing I thought when I heard."

Hetty nodded.

Gradually everyone drifted away and continued to chat in their own groups. When all were out of earshot, Lottie, with Hetty's help, told the family about Lucy Lacey's visit and how that was the real reason for Hetty's shock. The twins hung on to every word.

"But that's amazing," shrieked Kate, eyes like saucers.

"Wicked," agreed Vicki.

"But surely it's just a coincidence," laughed Bill, "I mean, reading broken biscuits, come on, that really does take the biscuit."

Zac chuckled.

"Not funny," scolded Sandra.

"Where does she live?" Kate asked, ignoring her father's scorn, "I imagine it's somewhere deep in the dark, dark woods."

Lottie smiled. "Not a bad guess. She lives in a cottage on moorland near to Pentrillick Woods."

"What's it called?" Vicki asked.

"Broomstick Cottage," suggested Bill.

Lottie frowned. "No, it's Wood Cottage."

"What was it she said again? I didn't quite grasp it just now." Sandra was clearly taken by the story.

"I wrote it down after she'd gone," said Hetty, "that's how I remember it. Lucy said: *I see yellow tulips in a shaft of sunlight. I see a lady cooking and she will get hurt. Other people will get hurt. Some will be deceitful. Things will go missing. Nothing will make sense. But you dear lady shall be unhurt for the lucky heather will protect you and your family.*"

"You won't hear me say this very often," admitted Sandra, "but I've gone all goosepimply."

"So have I," concurred Vicki.

Kate gasped. "And you bought yellow tulips, Mum."

"Which explains why Grandma and Auntie Het both looked like they'd seen a ghost when Mum handed them over." Zac looked and felt uneasy.

Bill, however, drained his glass and looked heavenwards. "Well, if Auntie Het and her family are safe we've nothing to worry about, have we?" He stood up. "Anyone fancy another drink?"

Later, Brett and Alina who were at Pentrillick House when the attempted murder took place arrived at the Crown and

Anchor where they-were questioned by all and sundry about the latest developments.

"Who are they and why are they always being fussed over?" Vicki asked, "It was the same the other night when I saw them."

"That's Brett Baker and his girlfriend, Alina," stated Hetty, feeling more relaxed after two glasses of wine.

"Who?"

"The script writer," said Zac, "The one who wrote *Murder at Mulberry Hall*. We were talking about him the other day."

"Oh, oh, I see. He's much older than I'd imagined and not as handsome either."

Kate giggled. "No, not a patch on the vicar."

"Does the vicar ever come in the pub?" Vicki asked, hopefully.

"Occasionally," answered Lottie, "he's a very sociable chap."

"With his wife?" Kate asked, her fingers crossed beneath the table.

"He's not married," laughed Zac, "but don't let that fact get your hopes up."

Chapter Ten

On Tuesday everything went back to normal after the Easter weekend. It was a lovely spring-like day and so in the morning the family drove to Marazion for a look over St Michaels' Mount. While they were out, Hetty took Albert for a walk and outside the post office she bumped into the vicar.

"Good morning, Sergeant," she laughed, "lovely day and I feel rather overdressed in coat, scarf *and* gloves."

"Good morning, Mrs Appleby, it is indeed. And like you've I'm also overdressed but then it has been rather chilly lately so we have a good excuse."

"On a more sombre note. Terrible business regarding Hazel Mitchell."

Vicar Sam sighed deeply. "Yes, it is and I'm very concerned about what happened to her. She rang me on Sunday evening, you see, and asked if I would pop in and see her. She didn't say why but I got the feeling she was worried about something. We agreed I'd call today because she was working yesterday. If only it had been the other way round. I pray she pulls through."

"Is she conscious?"

"No, far from it. One of the bullets damaged her brain and so they've put her in a medically induced coma."

Hetty gasped. "But that's dreadful."

"Yes, it is."

"So have you told the police about the call she made to you? I mean, it may well help with their enquiries."

"Yes, I have. I rang them as soon as I heard the news. They were very interested but I doubt it'll help much unless they can find someone who knew what was bothering her."

"Perhaps her children will know. I think she has two...grown up of course."

"Yes, she has but hopefully she'll recover soon and be able to tell the police all they need to know herself."

"We can but hope."

"And pray."

The family arrived back just after lunch and in the afternoon, Kate and Vicki announced they were going to walk down to the beach. This was because on the previous evening while in the Crown and Anchor, they had overheard someone saying they'd found a message in a bottle while out beachcombing that morning. Sadly though, the message was illegible as a little water had got inside and blurred the ink. The notion of beachcombing appealed to the girls and so just before three they set off with two carrier bags which they hoped to fill with treasures. However, when they arrived at the beach they found it was high water and so there was very little beach to explore.

"Bother," shouted Vicki, stamping her foot, "Dad said we ought to check the tide. It's so annoying when he's right. Now we'll have nothing to take back unless we hang around waiting for the tide to go out again and if we do wait anything we find will be sopping wet."

"Well, I suppose anything we found would still be wet even if the tide was out now. I mean it's hardly going to be dry after being in the sea for goodness knows how long."

"No, but it's a nice day so anything washed up would soon dry in the sun."

"Okay, you win." Kate looked across the beach. "I suppose we could explore those rocks over there. You never know the tide might have thrown something up there which the beachcombers will have missed."

"Yeah, you could be right. Worth a try anyway and better than doing nothing."

At the end of the beach the girls clamoured over the rocks. Kate found the going easy as she was wearing trainers. Vicki on the other hand wore flip-flops.

"Let's sit down and rest," suggested Kate, after they had walked for half an hour and found nothing other than an empty drinks can and water bottles which they had collected to dispose of in the recycling boxes at Primrose Cottage, "It's quite warm so it'll be nice to just sit and look at the sea."

Vicki readily agreed.

The girls sat side by side, legs outstretched with jeans rolled up to their knees to feel the warmth of the sun.

"I could happily fall asleep here," said Vicki, as she stifled a yawn, "the sea is so calming and it smells nice too." She removed her sunglasses and leaned back.

"I agree. I wish we lived near the sea because I like the sound it makes. I'd like to see it in the winter as well when it's really rough and the wind's howling."

"Well, I shall live by the sea when I'm older," declared Vicki, as she closed her eyes, "I might even come and live in Pentrillick."

"At the Vicarage?" Kate teased.

Vicki laughed. "Only in my dreams."

Because the tide was beginning to recede, they walked nearer to the sea on their way back and collected even more litter.

"Well, we're doing our bit for the environment," laughed Kate, as she picked up yet another plastic bottle, "so our efforts have not all been in vain."

Vicki suddenly stopped walking, clearly distracted as she pointed to her left. "I'm listening, Kate, really I am but what's that over there?"

"Where?"

"Over there by the triangular shaped rock. I can see something shining in the sunlight."

"Treasure," screamed Kate.

"Wow, be brilliant if it was."

Eagerly the girls scrambled towards the shiny object. Both gasped. For there beside a small rock pool lay not one but two brass candlesticks.

When the girls arrived back at Primrose Cottage with two bags; one full of litter the other holding the two brass candlesticks, Bill rang the police.

"I hope you managed to get the candlesticks into the bags without getting your fingerprints on them," said Sandra.

Kate looked indignant. "Oh, Mum, we're not stupid. Vicki held the bag open and I picked them up using the corner of my T-shirt."

"Good girls," Hetty was impressed.

"Did you notice whether or not they looked damaged?" Lottie asked.

"They're a bit mucky and one of them has a small dent but apart from that they seemed alright," stated Kate.

"That's a relief because I should imagine they cost a few bob."

"So do you think they're they the ones that were taken from the church?" Vicki asked, hopefully.

"They must be," said Lottie, taking another peek in the carrier bag, "I mean, I don't know for sure because I never looked at them closely when in church but it's too much of a coincidence for them not to be."

"But why take them if you're not going to keep them?" Sandra asked.

"Perhaps the thief panicked and threw them away because he couldn't risk having them found in his possession. I mean, I don't expect for a minute he thought he'd be interrupted on the night he took them," reasoned Bill.

"Interesting point," commented Lottie, "which means the fact he didn't expect to be interrupted rules out him being a local because locals would all know that half past seven on Wednesday is choir practice."

Hetty smiled. "Only ones that are church members, Lottie. I daresay most people in the pub wouldn't have a clue. In fact I'm not even sure that I would have known."

As Lottie was about to answer a car pulled up outside.

Zac leapt up and looked out of the window. "It's the police. I'll go and let them in."

"A penny for your thoughts," whispered Brett to Alina who sat on the hearth rug by his feet with her head resting on his lap.

"I was watching the flames in the fire. They're mesmerising and make me feel totally relaxed."

"Ah, so that's why you're so quiet."

"Yes, I'm tired as well. I think it must be the sea air." She lifted her head and looked into his eyes. "Don't you feel tired?"

"No, can't really say that I do and I think the reason for your tiredness is probably because you're worrying about your next job and that's quite understandable."

"Hmm, perhaps I am a little apprehensive but I don't think so."

"Do you fancy going down the pub for a drink? We could get a bite to eat as well as we've not eaten yet."

"Yes, if you like but I'm quite happy sitting here by the fire."

Brett laughed. "So you're feeling lazy and would rather stay?"

"If I'm honest, yes. I found the pub rather depressing last night. All the talk of the shooting was horrible especially when we were actually up there when it happened. The thought of that poor woman being shot makes me shudder. I didn't think things like that happened in Cornwall."

"Sadly crime happens everywhere, but certainly it's more prevalent in the big cities."

"Yes, I suppose you're right."

Brett dreamily twisted a lock of Alina's hair around his finger. "It's strange isn't it, that both of us earn our crusts through over-the-top drama; me with writing and you with acting, yet in reality it's pretty sordid and not something one would really like to be involved with. I could never be a copper."

"Nor me and you wouldn't be much good if you were. You're too soft hearted." Alina quietly laughed. "Even the baddies in *Murder at Mulberry Hall* are likable characters."

"And so are the people that play them."

"Do you really think so? I mean, I agree that Alex makes a brilliant dodgy hairstylist but I'm not so sure about his accomplice, Marlene. Admittedly she plays the part of his wife with flair but there's something about her that I don't like. I don't trust her."

Brett released her lock of hair and stroked it flat. "Hmm, can't see what you mean. Anywhere, there's a bottle of white in the fridge. Do you fancy a glass?"

Alina moved so that he could stand up. "Yes please and there's a pizza in the freezer as well so we'll have that a little later on."

Chapter Eleven

On Wednesday morning Hetty looked up from her laptop and groaned. "The car boot sale's been cancelled again, that's the third week running."

Bill moved over to the table where the yellow tulips gleamed in a shaft of sunlight and glanced out of the window. "But the weather looks quite nice and the sun's shining."

"Yes, it does but the problem is the field: it's water logged, you see, because of all the rain we've had."

"Oh, well, I'm sure we'll all find something else to do."

"Yes, but it would be nice to have gone because we want some new plants for the garden to replace the ones we lost during the cold spell."

"The Beast from the East," laughed, Kate, "it was wicked."

"Especially on the days it closed the school," added Vicki.

"We lost quite a few plants as well and we're used to cold winters," said Sandra, ignoring her daughters.

"But surely you can buy some more in all sorts of places," remarked Bill, "All the big stores and supermarkets will have them."

"Of course," agreed Hetty, as she closed down her laptop, "but we like looking at the car boot because we always feel we've got a bargain."

"Even if we haven't," Lottie added, "because they can sometimes work out more expensive."

Bill smiled. "Oh well, instead of going to the car boot sale you'll have to stay here and focus on trying to find out who attempted to murder the poor cook and who stole the candlesticks."

"And then threw them away," tutted Kate, "What a weirdo."

"We might just do that," agreed Hetty, as she tucked her laptop beneath the chair, "because although the attempted murder of poor old Hazel is a real mystery we do at least know now that Gideon was attacked because he disturbed a robber. At least we're pretty certain that's the reason."

Bill sat down on the sofa. "So do you think it's possible that the two incidents might be linked?"

"Probably but for the life of me I can't see how or why," conceded Hetty, "Having said that, it appears something had been bothering Hazel and she wanted to tell Vicar Sam about it. I met him yesterday while out walking Albert. Lottie and I have discussed it but we're none the wiser, are we Lottie?"

Lottie shook her head. "And then on top of everything else there's the theft we mentioned the other day which took place at Pentrillick House a few years back. I even wonder if that's in any way connected."

Hetty removed her reading glasses and returned them to their case. "It might be but I don't see how. It happened too long ago."

"Well, whatever, you're going to be very busy with three crimes to solve." Bill tried hard to keep the ridicule from his voice.

Hetty sighed. "Yes, and then on top of that I have my lines to learn for the play."

In the afternoon, Bill and Sandra decided to go with the girls to St. Ives. Zac had already gone into the village to meet Emma.

"Right," said Hetty, as they stood at the window and waved as the family's car drove off, "time to make up a list of suspects."

Lottie sat down. "I was wondering how long it would be before you suggested that."

Hetty took a notepad and pen from the drawer in the sideboard. "It's not going to be easy, is it? I mean, we know quite a lot of people now." She sat down at the table by the window. "We'll do men first."

"Are we going to list all the men we know or just ones who might be involved?"

"Just ones who might be involved. I mean, it'd be daft to include the likes of Vicar Sam and his dad, and of course Alex from next door and dear old Tommy."

"Good, it shouldn't take too long then especially since I can't even think of one name."

Hetty tutted. "Damn, neither can I."

"And another thing. Is the list for both incidents or are you doing separate ones for each?"

Hetty groaned. "Trust you to be awkward. I hadn't thought of that. What do you think?"

"I'd just do one list for both crimes because I don't think we'll be able to come up with enough names for two so we'd end up duplicating them."

"Very true, and for now we'll forget about the robbery at Pentrillick House because it's thought that was done by professionals anyway." She wrote suspects at the top of the page. "Right, Lottie, who goes on first?"

Lottie frowned. "I wonder if it might in some way be connected to the drama group. I mean, Gideon's attack occurred after that first meeting."

"But why? Hazel Mitchell didn't belong to the drama group and nor did Gideon."

"True, but I think Kitty was going to ask Gideon to help with the music and Hazel Mitchell was a cook and it's the cook who gets murdered in the play."

A look of horror crossed Hetty's face. "You don't think I'm in danger do you, Lottie? Me being the cook in the play, I mean."

"I hardly think so unless you know something someone might want you to keep quiet about."

"You're right. That's a relief and of course I have the heather to protect me anyway."

"Hmm, yes," Lottie couldn't think of anything else to say.

Hetty tapped the pen on the notepad. "Come on, we're wasting time. Let's get back to the list of suspects."

"Well, I think the first person you need to write down is Pickle the Poacher after all he was on the Pentrillick Estate on the night of the robbery a few years back. I know we're not focusing on that but he was there. Also he was on the estate when Hazel was shot. What's more it was him who told everyone at the pub about Gideon so he might have been lurking around in the churchyard."

"Hmm, you could be right. He's certainly a character of interest but how do you know he was at Pentrillick House when Hazel was shot?"

"I heard someone say when we were in the pub the other day. I can't remember who but apparently he was up there with one of his sons who had popped down for the Easter weekend with his wife and two children."

"Hmm, well if he had family with him he's hardly likely to have shot Hazel, is he? But I'll put him down anyway."

"How about Brett?"

"Brett!" shouted Hetty, "Why on earth would he be involved?"

Lottie shrugged her shoulders. "Because he's here I suppose."

"Well, certainly he was here when Hazel was shot but I don't think he was when Gideon was attacked."

"Yes, he was. He and Alina arrived last Tuesday or Wednesday for Easter. What's more, he wrote a play in which there is a robbery and a cook is murdered."

"And that's two very good reasons why it's not him." Hetty laughed, "He'd be crackers to write about crimes he's committed or about to commit, if you see what I mean."

"Does seem a bit of a coincidence though." Lottie tried to back up her suggestion with a motive but realised it was unlikely that Brett knew Gideon or Hazel Mitchell anyway.

"Okay," said Hetty, "I'll put him down if it makes you happy and then let's move on."

"How about Ian?" Lottie suggested, "You know the chap who's going to do the lighting for the play. I think he looks a bit suspicious. Not that I've ever had reason to speak to him."

Hetty added his name to the list. "I can't see why but he'll do for now."

"And then there's that chap Christopher who does guided tours at Pentrillick House. I think his name was Christopher."

"Hmm, he'd certainly be in the know as far as the robbery is concerned and he would have known Hazel as well." Hetty wrote down his name and tapped the pen against her teeth. "I'm just trying to think of that woman's name. You know, the one with the annoying voice who also does guided tours."

"Yes, I know who you mean but I can't remember her name either."

"I'll just write down tour woman for now."

"We've gone onto the women then?"

"Well yes, because we're not getting very far with the men."

Lottie laughed. "And I don't think we'll do any better with women. Having said that write down Alina."

"Alina," gasped Hetty. "I can't see her having the strength to have knocked out Gideon. Those church candlesticks are quite heavy and I reckon if she lifted one high enough to hit someone over the head, she'd snap in two."

"Well, she's the only female I can think of that I don't really know."

Hetty frowned. "I've mixed feelings about this one but how about Lucy Lacey?"

"I thought you liked her because of the lucky heather."

"I do, it's just she said about people getting hurt, being deceitful and things going missing so perhaps she's involved."

Lottie shook her head. "No, I don't think so. Try and think of someone less unusual and more iffy."

"Aha, yes" squealed Hetty, "I know someone who fits that description. Marlene. She's an iffy looking character if ever I saw one."

"Is she? Why?"

"Well, um, well, I don't really know. She just is."

"In other words, you don't like her."

"No, I suppose I don't."

Lottie laughed. "I hope it's not because she's very good at playing the hairstylist's wife."

Hetty felt her face turn pink. "Could be. In fact she's too good and that's probably why I don't trust her. And another thing…she lives next door to Gideon and Debbie."

"Now that is a good reason because I've heard through Kitty that Marlene and Gideon don't get on too well because he's complained to her about the loud music her teenage children play until late at night."

"Really! She goes to the top of the list then."

"And don't forget her husband," said Lottie, "as I daresay he's troublesome too."

"Alright, but what's his name?"

"Gary. I know that because she mentioned him at the last meeting."

"Did she? Why was that?"

"She was telling someone about him and saying how he used to be in the army."

The colour drained from Hetty's face. "In which case, he'll know how to use a gun."

On Thursday morning, Hetty and Lottie having made a list of suspects none of whom they thought were guilty of either crime decided to take a trip to Pentrillick House. It was after all, the location of the attempted assassination of Hazel Mitchell and also of the robbery in 2013; therefore they reasoned it had to be well worth a visit. Sandra and Bill went with them as the girls were out for the day with Zac and Emma: all four having gone to the theme park in Helston.

"I suppose the girls having found the candlesticks means the police have a sound motive now for the attack on Gideon," Sandra said, as she turned her head from the front seat of the car where she sat beside Bill.

Lottie nodded. "I should imagine so as I can't think of any other reason for Gideon's assault."

Bill looked at the reflection of his mother in the rear view mirror. "That's a good point but why didn't the burglar just run off? I think I'm right in saying Gideon didn't see his face so there was no need to injure the poor man."

"We gather a mobile phone was left on the vestry floor so the burglar would have needed to collect it otherwise he'd be traced."

"Ah, I see. That makes sense."

Sandra scowled. "But what apart from the candlesticks might a burglar hope to find in a church to steal? I know it was commonplace once upon a time for offertory boxes to be broken into but if he was disturbed in the vestry it looks like the possibility of that isn't valid because if I remember correctly they're usually situated by the church door."

"Yes, that's puzzled us too," said Lottie, "but when we spoke about it to Sam he told us the communion chalice they use is silver, unusual and valuable. Apparently it's quite old and was donated to the church by a well-wisher so the thief might have been after that and just took the candlesticks rather than have nothing. The chalice isn't in the chest though: it's hidden in a locked-up cupboard near the organ."

Bill chuckled. "Perhaps someone fancied a drink and they were looking for the communion wine."

"Hmm, even that's possible," Hetty agreed.

"But surely it's non-alcoholic," said Sandra.

Lottie shook her head. "No, far from it. It's fortified but I understand it mustn't be more than eighteen percent proof."

Sid was glad to stand up after having spent twenty minutes bent double beneath one of the large stainless steel sinks in the lakeside café at Pentrillick House. The sink had been blocked but now it was clear and he was keen to get outside in the fresh air away from the heat of the kitchen. After washing his hands, he picked up a complimentary cream doughnut and a mug of coffee, made for him by the café manageress, and carried both outside intending to sit on one of the benches overlooking the lake. However, as he walked away from the café he saw the area was cordoned off and that several police officers, along with numerous divers, stood near to the water's edge; on the lake was a boat. Not to be outdone, Sid sat down on the grass as near to the cordon as possible and watched the boys in blue at work.

When Hetty, Lottie, Bill and Sandra arrived at Pentrillick House the first person they saw whom they recognised was Tess Dobson who had just dropped off Crown and Anchor leaflets to top up the information rack in the vestibule of the house.

"Tess," called Lottie, beckoning her to join them, "allow me to introduce you to my son, Bill and his wife, Sandra."

"Ah, yes, I saw you in the pub the other night but didn't make the connection." She held out her hand. "Delighted to meet you both. I assume you've come down for Easter."

"Yes," said Bill, "and it seems there is a lot happening in the village just like the last time we were here two years ago."

"Never a dull moment in village life," laughed Tess.

"There certainly isn't in this village," agreed Hetty.

"You seem very perky this afternoon, Tess," commented Lottie, "Have you come across some interesting gossip by any chance?"

Tess giggled. "Well, actually, yes, and for that reason I'm glad to have bumped into you. You see I've just this very moment discovered, through chatting to one of the security guards in the house, that police divers have found something of interest on the bottom of the lake. We assume it's the gun but will have to wait for confirmation. I understand the police are still down there and the lake is cordoned off."

"Really, now that is interesting," gasped Hetty, "but I suppose if it is the gun the fact it's been in the water for some time will mean there won't be any traces of fingerprints left now."

"Well, I shouldn't think there would be anyway," scoffed Lottie, "everyone knows that any baddie worth his salt would wear gloves."

Hetty sighed. "True, I suppose."

"Have you any idea of the sequence of events?" Lottie asked Tess, "I mean, who found Hazel and stuff like that?"

"Yes, it was Christopher the tour guide who found her. He was in the next room having a tea break before the next tour when he heard two shots. He dashed out into the passageway and found Hazel slumped in the kitchen doorway."

"Hmm, I suppose that rules him out then," groaned Hetty, begrudgingly.

Tess laughed. "Surely you never suspected him. Chris is lovely and he wouldn't hurt a fly. What's more, he and Hazel got on really well together."

"So what exactly did he do when he found Hazel?" Hetty asked, eager for every little detail, "I mean, did he ring the police, give chase or what?"

"He rang Tristan on his mobile and then Tristan rang the police," answered Tess, "He certainly didn't give chase because there was no-one in the kitchen to chase."

"I see, so by the time the police arrived the gunman would have been long gone," mused Hetty.

Lottie shook her head. "No, he wouldn't have left the premises straight away because at some point he must have walked down to the lake and chucked the gun in and it'd take a good five minutes to walk down there."

"Assuming it is the gun that the police have discovered," reasoned Sandra.

"Good point," agreed Lottie, "we shall have to wait and see."

After they saw Tess, Bill and Sandra went on a tour of the house. Hetty and Lottie, eager to see the police activity headed down towards the lake. On their way they met Samantha Liddicott-Treen.

"Dreadful business about your cook," said Hetty, feeling it necessary to commiserate, "We're so sorry, you must feel awful."

"We do," sighed Samantha, "and poor Tristan is distraught. He blames himself and says we should have better security."

"Oh, but he mustn't feel guilty," said Lottie, "No-one could have foreseen this."

"That's what I tell him but it doesn't help. He was very fond of Hazel and of course it makes him feel worse knowing that she had made an apple pie for our dinner that evening because she knew it was his favourite. Fortunately it was saved from incineration because a police officer noticed the smell and he had the sense to take in from the oven. We weren't allowed in the kitchen, you see. Not at that time and I must admit I don't like going in there now. Poor Tristan, the apple pie is still there in the fridge and as much as he wants to eat it he can't because he said it doesn't seem right."

Hetty had to smile. "But surely that's the very thing he should do because if not when she recovers Hazel will be most unhappy to learn her effort went to waste."

"I like your positivity."

"I'm a very positive person."

Hetty was delighted when she heard Samantha laugh.

On Thursday afternoon, Brett drove Alina to Penzance station to catch a train to London. When he arrived back in the village, he parked the car by Sea View Cottage and then walked to the Crown and Anchor. After he bought his drink he saw Robert who had just finished his lunch.

"Mind if I join you?"

"Of course not. Sit down."

"Thanks."

"On your own?"

"Yes, Alina's had to go back to London. They start filming a new television drama series on Monday that she's in so she needs to get ready for that."

"Very nice. Does she have a very big part?"

"Big enough for it to be worth doing but not big enough to cause her sleepless nights, if you see what I mean." Brett took a sip of his beer and placed the glass on the table.

"Well I get the impression she's a very talented lady who hopefully will eventually make the big time."

"Hmm, I'm not sure that she wants to though. She certainly doesn't want Hollywood and all that stuff. She's very much a home bird. As long as she's making a decent living, she's happy."

"Good for her. There's a lot to be said for that."

"Very true," Brett agreed, "and I'm glad I've run into you because I've been giving some thought to the play and wonder, do you think it might be a good idea to make a couple of small alterations to it?"

"How do you mean?"

"I'm thinking perhaps have someone other than the cook murdered. It just seems so tasteless after what happened at Pentrillick House on Monday. And then there's the fact Mrs Appleby is bludgeoned with a candlestick which seems undiplomatic when rumour has it that the same weapon was used in the attack on Gideon Elms."

"Ah, two very good points. Not sure what to say about the candlestick but I know Hetty would be terribly upset if she wasn't the fatality."

"She could still be the victim but have her as someone other than the cook."

"Such as?"

"I don't know. A nanny or something like that."

Robert smiled. "But our hairstylist only has one child and she's grown up."

Brett laughed. "Yes, good point."

"Let's see how it goes. I mean, if Hazel pulls through then we'll leave it as it is but if not…well, we'll give Hetty a different role without having to change her words. As for the candlestick, if Gideon takes a turn for the worse we'll come up with a different weapon but I don't think that will be necessary because I've heard he's doing very well."

"Okay, so for now we'll carry on as normal."

"Yes, Hetty stays as the cook and a candlestick remains the weapon."

When Brett and Robert left the Crown and Anchor they walked partway home together along the main street until Robert turned off near the church into Honeysuckle Close where he lived in the very last bungalow. Horticulture wasn't a subject that interested Robert so apart from his driveway, tarmacked with flecks of white, the entire garden was laid to lawns with the occasional shrub here and there. The lawns, however, were immaculate but that was because he paid Percy Pickering to come in once a week to tend them.

The interior of the bungalow was minimalistic. The walls were painted white throughout and the furniture was simple and plain. The surfaces were devoid of ornaments and the only splash of colour on the kitchen wall was a calendar with pictures of dogs in various countryside locations. Not something Robert would have chosen but he rather liked it because it reminded him of Wendy, his girlfriend of several years who was in the Royal Navy and away at sea. It was Wendy's desire to have a dog when she came out of the Navy which wouldn't be long, just another two years until she reached the end of her service.

Robert was a financial adviser. Self-employed and he worked from home. He liked it that way. His time was his own which meant he could work around his hobby, the Pentrillick Players.

Chapter Twelve

On Friday morning, fourteen year old Jeremy Liddicott-Treen, home from school for the Easter holiday, sat on the path which ran around the lake at Pentrillick House and dropped pebbles into the water. He was angry: angry and upset. In his opinion Hazel Mitchell was the best cook in the world; everything she made was delicious especially her ginger biscuits which were the envy of his school friends when he received them in the post from home. She was also friendly, funny and always made time to talk to him which was one of the reasons he looked forward to coming home from boarding school. She was like a grandmother to him or an aunt or a godmother and he didn't know how he was going to cope if she did not survive.

"It's bad enough her being seriously ill," he told an inquisitive duck, "but to have been shot, here in our kitchen, it's too much. And who can have done it and why?"

The duck on realising he had nothing edible to offer swam off. Jeremy clambered to his feet and began to walk away from the lake: the lake in which the hateful gun had been found. He looked up at the house and cursed the fact there was no CCTV in the grounds which meant there was no way of seeing who amongst the crowds had tossed the gun away on Easter Monday. Admittedly there were cameras in the house but they were focused on the tour route and none were anywhere near the kitchen.

As he walked towards the house he wondered how best to spend the day. He knew that if Mrs Mitchell were to see him she would tick him off for moping. Always look on the bright side, she'd say and every cloud has a silver lining. He sighed: he wasn't going to see her though, was he? Not today or tomorrow or possibly ever again.

He passed a bench and on it sat a young woman reading. He thought perhaps that's what he might do. Finish the book he had started on Easter Sunday evening. His shoulders slumped. But that was the book he'd told Mrs Mitchell about on Monday morning just hours before she was shot. She'd been really interested when he'd told her what had happened in the first few chapters. It was a detective story and there was a man in it who everyone thought to be a real charmer but Jeremy suspected he was actually a confidence trickster. Mrs Mitchell had laughed when he said that but she still wanted him to tell her how it ended when he'd finished it. What was it she had said when he mentioned a confidence trickster? He remembered – there's so much good in the worst of us and so much bad in the best of us. Jeremy smiled as he walked up the steps and into the house. Typical Mrs Mitchell, looking on the bright side as usual.

On Friday afternoon, Hetty and Lottie took a walk down to the charity shop to see if they had any wigs because Hetty had decided her character in the play, Mrs Appleby, ought to have short grey hair. Maisie and Daisy, on duty when they arrived were both amused by Hetty's request.

"But why do you think Mrs Appleby should have grey hair?" asked Maisie.

"I don't know but I just feel she should. Anyway, I want her to look different to me and a wig seems a good way of achieving that. Might help me get into character as well."

"Fair enough," said Daisy, "and as it happens we do have several wigs. They're out the back along with stuff we put aside for fancy dress on New Year's Eve. I'll go and fetch them."

"Brilliant, thanks," chuckled Hetty, gleefully rubbing her hands.

As Daisy disappeared into the stockroom, a car pulled up on the pavement, the shop door opened and Brett Baker walked in carrying two large cardboard boxes. "I'm hoping you can make use of this stuff," he said, as he put the boxes down on the floor. "I've more in the car, I'll just go and get them."

"Wow, this should be interesting," exclaimed Maisie.

Lottie nodded. "Looks like he's been having a clear out."

"I have," confirmed Brett as he returned and dropped three more boxes on the floor. "I bought the cottage along with its contents to save the vendor coming down here to dispose of it. I've been meaning to go through it for ages and I've finally got round to it. I'm keeping all the furniture but this is stuff I don't need. I hope it's of use to you; there's all sorts of odds and sods."

Maisie glanced at the boxes. "Oh, it definitely will and it's kind of you to think of us. We're very grateful and I'm sure, were they able to speak, then the animals it will help would thank you too."

"My pleasure. Glad to have got it done, now I'll be able to go back to London next week with a clear conscience."

As he left, Daisy emerged from the stockroom with a carrier bag. "Ow, a delivery. I love looking through donations."

"From Brett," said Maisie, peeking into a box of pots and pans, "I see you found the wigs."

"Yes, I did." Daisy tipped the wigs onto the counter. "And as you can see we have two grey ones. Try them on if they take your fancy, Het. There's a mirror over by the dress rack."

While Hetty tried on the wigs, Maisie and Daisy unpacked the first box looked on by Lottie.

"What do you think?" Hetty asked, stepping away from the mirror, her head a mass of grey curls.

"I wouldn't recognise you," said Maisie, genuinely surprised. "It looks brilliant."

Daisy nodded. "Yes, quite a transformation."

"Now we know what you'd look like if you didn't dye your hair." Lottie was amazed how much Hetty looked like their late grandmother but thought it best not to say so.

"Thank you, I'll just try the other then you can tell me which you think looks best."

The style of the second was straight and very short. The ladies unanimously gave it the thumbs down and so Hetty opted for the curls.

"Anything interesting in Brett's boxes?" she asked as Maisie took her money.

"Books in this one," said Daisy holding up a copy of Charles Dickens' *Great Expectations*.

Lottie laughed. "Hopefully that book title is a good omen."

In the evening, the family went to the Crown and Anchor and much to the delight of the girls, Vicar Sam was there with his parents who were due to return home the following day.

"Have you managed to distribute all the biscuits?" Hetty asked Penelope while her husband and the vicar played a game of pool.

"Most of them, thank goodness. We've left a few boxes with Sammy which we've asked him to pass on. We'd have done it ourselves but the fortnight seems to have gone ridiculously fast and we must go home tomorrow because Michael has a hospital appointment on Monday."

"Oh dear, nothing serious I hope."

"No, no, just a routine check-up. His heart's a bit dodgy but it's all under control."

"That's good and again thank you for the biscuits, the ones I've had so far have been delicious."

Penelope laughed. "I'm pleased to hear that because we have every intention of coming back at the end of next month so we can see the play whatever it's called and we'll no doubt be able to fill the car boot with them again by then."

"*Murder at Mulberry Hall*," said Hetty, "that's the name of the play."

"Sounds wonderful."

"It is and great fun to be in."

"So Sammy said. It must be doing him good because I've never seen him as happy as he seems to be now. I even wondered if he might have a girlfriend but he says not. Which is a shame because I'd like grandchildren before I get too old to play with them."

On Saturday morning, Kate and Vicki announced they were going for a walk.

"Well don't get lost," teased Bill.

"We're only going along the coast path," tutted Kate, "so can hardly lose our way."

"Which way are you going?" Lottie asked.

"We thought towards the east," replied Vicki.

"Good choice and that way you'll pass the old lifeboat house. It's a holiday home now but still quite fascinating to see the way it's nestled between the cliffs and it doesn't stretch the imagination too much to visualise how it might have worked in its heyday."

The girls left Primrose Cottage just after nine. The morning was overcast but occasionally the sun managed to peep briefly through the clouds. The well-worn coastal path was dry but the surrounding bracken, gorse and greenery was still damp from early morning drizzle. When they reached the old lifeboat house they stopped and sat down on a boulder. There was a car parked near to the property and people appeared to be packing things into the boot.

"They must have come down for Easter and now they're going home," said Kate, "Poor things. I'm glad we've still got another week."

"Same here. We don't want to leave our vicar just yet."

"No but today we have another mission to complete which I think is quite exciting."

"And scary," laughed Vicki.

"Come on let's not waste time." Kate sprang to her feet.

They continued walking until the old lifeboat house was no longer visible and soon reached the relics of an old mine.

"Creepy," whispered Vicki as she peeped inside what was left of the remaining walls.

"I wonder if *Poldark* is filmed here," giggled Kate. "If it is we might see Ross come riding by."

"Hardly," tutted Vicki, "mines were still very much in use back in Poldark's day so they're hardly going to film by a relic."

"Yes, of course. Come on, we must be nearly there now."

After a few more dips and bends in the path they saw trees not too far away.

"That has to be Pentrillick Woods," reasoned Vicki waving her hand.

"Definitely but I can't see any houses and she's supposed to live on moorland between the sea and the edge of the woods."

"Well it's quite hilly along there so her house might be tucked in a dip."

Shortly afterwards they saw smoke and so to get a better view climbed onto a fence which ran alongside the path.

"I can see it," squealed Kate, excitedly waving her hand, "look over by that telegraph pole but the coast path doesn't appear to go anywhere near it."

"There must be a lane nearby or something like that. Come on, let's see if we can find it."

Kate frowned. "But if a lane runs by it, it isn't going to run down as far as the coastal path, is it? There would be no point."

"Damn, no. It looks like we're going to have to go over fields then. Let's find a meadow because we don't want to walk over crops and stuff like that."

On reaching a grass field they climbed over the fence and keeping to the side by a hedge they headed towards the cottage. When they reached a five bar gate they looked to the other side where a dirt track ran back inland. Eagerly they climbed the gate and followed the track which to their delight ran past the cottage.

"What do we do now?" Kate asked, as they crouched on a grass verge.

"Go and knock on the door I suppose."

"But what if she's a witch? I'm suddenly scared."

Vicki laughed. "You coward. Come on there are two of us and from what we've heard she's quite small." Vicki stood and then pulled her sister to her feet.

"She might not be in," said Kate, half hoping that was the case.

Vicki opened a small gate with Wood Cottage notched into the green paintwork. "Of course she'll be in because according to Auntie Hetty she hardly ever goes out."

On either side of the path heather grew in various shades but white was the most prominent colour. Near to the house, birds sang on the leafless branches of a pear tree and over by an old well a garden swing dangled from a brightly coloured frame.

"Have you got the pound coins safe?" Vicki asked.

"Yes, of course."

"Good, come on it'll only take a minute." With arms linked the twins walked along the twisted path which led up to the small front door.

"It's like the gingerbread house in Hansel and Gretel," whispered Kate.

Vicki giggled. "Well if she has a large stone oven keep well away from it."

Nervously Vicki knocked on the door. All was silent until they heard a cough from inside the house. Slowly the door opened.

Lucy Lacey, wearing a spotted dress, long cardigan and slippers with a bobble on the front, smiled. "Come in, come in, my dears," she said, "I've been expecting you."

It was half past one when the twins arrived back at Primrose Cottage.

"Ah, we were about to send out a search party," joked Bill, as he swallowed the last mouthful of cheese on toast, "It's not like you two to be late for lunch."

"Sorry but we lost track of time," giggled Vicki.

"And I expect you're hungry," said Lottie.

"A bit," admitted Kate.

Lottie stood up. "What would you like?"

"A ham sandwich, please," said Kate, "with a little bit of mustard."

Vicki nodded. "And the same for me."

"I'll make them," Sandra sprang to her feet, "you sit down, Mum. You've done enough for one day."

"Okay, thank you, love."

"So what have you been up to?" Bill asked, as Sandra left the room, "It must be something exciting because you both have shining eyes."

Vicki took a sprig of white heather from the pocket of her jeans and held it in front of her face. Kate followed suit.

Hetty gasped. "You've seen Lucy Lacey. Where? According to Kitty she seldom goes out."

"We went to her cottage," blurted Vicki, excitedly, "it's really dinky. There's a sitting room, a tiny kitchen and bathroom downstairs and then two little bedrooms upstairs. She let us have a look round while she made us cups of tea."

"And the walls in the house are all crooked," gushed Kate, "and she's got loads and loads of heather growing in her garden."

"There's also a swing in the garden and an old well," added Vicki, "and in the upstairs rooms of the house the floors are crooked too."

"There was a crooked man, and he walked a crooked mile,
He found a crooked sixpence against a crooked stile;
He bought a crooked cat which caught a crooked mouse,
And they all lived together in a little crooked house," Bill recited.

"Well remembered," applauded Hetty, "even if it is inappropriate."

"I can't believe you went to her house," Lottie looked displeased, "Whatever made you do that?"

"Very silly," scolded Bill, feeling perhaps he ought to take a more serious stance, "you should never call on strangers like that."

"But...but we wanted some heather, like Auntie Hetty because it brought her good luck and got her the part she wanted in the play." Kate's mouth turned upside-down.

Hetty frowned at her sister and then at Bill. "Well, no harm done," she said, "and I suppose it is my fault for going on about the heather and how Lucy's broken biscuit prediction seems to have come true." She stood up and gave both girls a hug, "What's more, Lottie Burton, it's the sort of thing we'd have done when we were young."

Bill laughed. "Yes, and I suppose if I'm honest I might have done the same myself. Sit down girls."

"So, what was the house like?" Hetty was keen to know every detail, "Apart from being crooked that is."

"As we said it's dinky," reiterated Vicki, "but it feels lovely and cosy."

"And from the outside it looks like the witch's house in Hansel and Gretel, "added Kate.

Zac laughed. "So does she have a black cat?"

"No," snapped Kate, "well, she has a cat but it's not black, it's white."

"No doubt called Merlin," chortled Bill.

"Actually, he's called George," said Vicki.

"But what's the house like inside?" Hetty asked.

"Dead old fashioned," giggled Kate, "and it smells of lavender or something like that."

"And on one of the walls is a huge aerial picture of Pentrillick House and the surrounding area including her cottage." Vicki stretched out her arms to demonstrate the size of the picture, "It nearly covers the whole wall."

"She gave us tea and biscuits," gabbled Kate, "and like she did you, Auntie Hetty, she told our fortunes. It was great fun. We loved it, didn't we, Vick?"

Vicki nodded. "Yes."

"So what did she say?" Bill was intrigued.

"I'm going to be a police officer," stated Kate with gusto.

"And I'm going to be a history teacher," added Vicki, with very little enthusiasm.

"You're going to be a history teacher," repeated Sandra as she entered the room with two plates of sandwiches, "but you don't even like history. In fact you always say you hate it."

"Hmm, well I suppose over the next few years I'll discover I like it."

"They've had their fortunes told," Bill chuckled, "by the mysterious Lucy Lacey."

"Who isn't mysterious at all," cried Kate, "she's really lovely."

"And she has a white cat called George," said Zac.

Sandra handed a plate to each of the girls and then sat down. "So where did you see her? I got the impression she seldom goes out."

"They went to her house would you believe." Lottie answered for the girls because they both had their mouths full.

Sandra tutted. "Poor lady. She must have been surprised when you two turned up."

"Well, that's the strange thing," muttered Kate, as she swallowed a mouthful of sandwich, "she said, come in, come in, my dears, I've been expecting you."

"You didn't tell us that." Hetty felt giddy.

"That's because I've only just remembered," said Kate.

"And not only was she expecting us," giggled Vicki, "but she knew who we were."

"But how?" Sandra was staggered.

Kate shrugged her shoulders.

"Apparently she can sense when things are going to happen," said Vicki, "because she's a telepathic soothsayer but she laughed when she called herself that so I don't know whether or not she was pulling our legs."

Chapter Thirteen

"I was just wondering," commented Hetty, who had arrived early at the drama group meeting along with Kitty and Lottie on Monday evening, "if some of the money raised from the play performances could go towards decorating the church. Some of the walls are looking quite shabby and could really do with a lick of paint."

Robert sighed as he put out a row of chairs. "Well we don't really raise much money after expenses and what we do make usually goes towards our Christmas party."

"Oh, I see, yes, of course."

"And our Christmas party is the highlight of the year for many," laughed Kitty, as she removed her coat, "as you've witnessed these last two years."

Hetty smiled. "Yes, I can understand that. Never mind, it was just a thought."

"I suppose we could do something else to raise the money," said Kitty, noting the look of disappointment on Hetty's face, "a fete perhaps or a sponsored walk."

Brett who was at a loose end because Alina was in London, had also arrived early and listened quietly to what was being discussed. "No need," he said, after brief consideration, "I'm getting quite fond of this village and although I'm not a church-goer I do accept that it's an important part of the community so I'd be more than happy to pay all costs for it to be decorated."

"Would you really?" Hetty was overcome by his generosity.

Brett smiled. "Yes, of course but I don't want to make a song and dance of it. Perhaps we can keep it amongst ourselves."

"So who would we get to do it?"

"Leave it with me," suggested Brett, "and I'll have a quiet word with Sam when he gets here. He's bound to know someone but please let my involvement go no further than these four walls."

"Mum's the word," whispered Hetty. Kitty, Lottie and Robert agreed.

After the meeting Hetty and Lottie followed Marlene to the pub trying with every step to hear what she was saying to Robert and Brett with whom she had tagged along as they walked down the street, but to their annoyance, they were too far behind to catch more than the occasional word. Kitty wasn't with them because she wanted to speak to Vicar Sam about church business and so told them to go on ahead.

When they arrived at the Crown and Anchor, they saw Marlene's husband, Gary, sitting at the bar talking to a man who was not familiar to either of the sisters. Marlene, however, clearly knew him for she promptly made a bee-line towards her husband where the unfamiliar man kissed her on the cheek. Keen to know who he was Hetty and Lottie sought out Tess.

"That's Paul, you know the chap who took a leading part in our drama group's production in 2016 when he was here for the summer."

"Ah, the mystery chap who no-one knows much about," gasped Hetty.

Tess nodded. "That's right."

"He's very handsome," said Lottie, struck by his thick, dark hair and striking features, "he reminds me of my late husband when he was a young man."

"So is he here for a holiday?" Hetty asked.

"No, apparently he is here for the summer and like before is renting a house somewhere."

"In the village?" Hetty was eager for any little detail.

"I expect so but I don't know for sure. He only arrived last night."

"Oh, pity he didn't get here a bit earlier," said Lottie, "then he could have been in *Murder at Mulberry Hall.*"

"I said that to him just now," laughed Tess, "but he said he has rather a heavy workload so is quite happy to watch our efforts instead."

Robert was clearly delighted to see Paul and introduced him to Brett. The men then moved to sit at a table in the corner of the bar near to the piano and chatted happily together for the rest of the evening.

"Paul seemed a nice chap," commented Lottie as the sisters walked up Long Lane with Kitty on their way home.

"I thought so too," Kitty agreed. "I wasn't involved with the drama group in 2016 when he was here because I had a bad back but I saw his performance and it was quite superb."

"In which case," said Hetty, turning over thoughts in her mind, "if it's acknowledged that he's a very good actor, I wonder, is he a nice chap or just pretending that he is?"

"Oh, Het, surely you're not suggesting he might in any way be involved in the unsavoury events of late," tutted Lottie.

"Hmm, no but it pays to keep an open mind."

"But he's only just got here," laughed Kitty, "and apparently knew nothing of our troubles until tonight. I overheard Robert telling him."

"Only just arrived at Polquillick, yes, but he might have been staying elsewhere in the county and we're unaware of it."

Lottie sighed. "Someone else to add to the list then."

On Wednesday, Gideon came out of hospital and so in the afternoon, after first ringing to make sure that it was alright, Hetty and Lottie went to visit him. They found him in the sitting room beside the fire with his feet resting on a stool. While

Debbie, his wife, made cups of tea, they asked how he was feeling.

"Not bad at all and to be honest I feel a lot better for being home. My old head's a bit sore but then that's hardly surprising, is it?"

"No," agreed Lottie, "and I must admit you look a lot better than I thought you would."

"Are you disappointed?"

Lottie looked horrified. "No, no, of course not."

Gideon laughed. "I was only pulling your leg."

Hetty briefly puzzled over how best to ask about the attack and in the end decided to be blunt. "Can you actually remember anything about the night you were knocked on the head?"

"I can't remember anything useful, more's the shame. But just before I was hit I heard a squeak and it reminded me of the ball which belonged to our dear old dog."

"You used to have a dog, I didn't know that," interrupted Lottie, "what breed was it?"

"A Springer Spaniel and his name was Derek. He died about six months before we moved down here. Bless his heart, he was a lovely dog and great company."

"Oh that's sad. I am sorry."

"So what happened after the squeak?" Hetty was a little annoyed by the deviation.

"It was followed by a strong smell of scent or aftershave. I wish I could identify it, but I can't," Gideon chuckled, "never been a great one for recognising scents. Ask our Debbie."

Hetty's hopes were raised. "Ah, but would you recognise it if you came across it again?"

Lottie laughed. "What are you suggesting, Het, that we drag Gideon along to the chemists and get him sniffing all the aftershave and perfume testers?"

"Well, no, but now you come to mention it that's a very good idea."

"Certainly a novel proposal," laughed Gideon, "but would it achieve anything other than getting us thrown out of the chemists?"

Hetty sighed. "No I suppose not because it's already common knowledge you remember a scent of some sort so I daresay the person who attacked you has already chucked the bottle, can or whatever in the bin."

"I tell you what I would recognise though and that's the ringtone on my assailant's phone. I'm pretty good when it comes to music but the trouble is I'd never heard the tune before so can't say what it was."

"Could you hum it?" Hetty was desperate for any information that might help.

Gideon shook his head. "Sadly not because although I'd recognise it if I heard it again, I can't remember it. I hope that makes sense."

Hetty nodded. "Yes, it does."

"Did the police find any fingerprints?" Lottie asked.

"No, because there wouldn't have been any. My assailant wore gloves that I do remember."

Hetty sat forward in her chair. "Ah, what colour were they?"

"Black but I couldn't say whether they were knitted, leather or whatever. It all happened too quickly."

"So really the police don't have much to go on. What a shame."

"Yes, and it appears nothing was taken apart from the candlesticks so at least I stopped the thief getting away with whatever they were hoping to find and I believe the candlesticks have been found anyway."

"Yes, they have. My granddaughters found them discarded on the rocks at the end of the beach."

Gideon tutted. "I hope they weren't damaged."

"No, they appear to be fine apart from a small dent. When the police handed them back Kitty took them away to give them a good polish so they're as good as new now."

"Good old Kitty," laughed Gideon, "she's a good sort and she tells me the choir's anthem on Easter Sunday was perfect."

"It was and no doubt the choir members were determined it would be as a tribute to you," said Lottie in earnest.

Hetty agreed. "Yes, and I know they'd love to find out who attacked you. I've heard they were all pretty shaken when they arrived for the practice and found out what had happened."

"So I've been told. Several came to visit me in hospital, even some of the youngsters. I must admit their thoughtfulness brought a tear to my eyes."

"That's nice to hear," said Lottie, "and I bet they all wish they'd arrived a little earlier and caught the thief before he absconded."

Hetty sighed. "That would have been nice. As it is I don't think this crime will ever be solved."

"I'm inclined to agree and the police have enough on their hands at the moment trying to find out who attempted to murder poor Hazel Mitchell." Gideon tutted, "Shocking do that."

"Did you know her at all?" Lottie asked.

"Not really, we always greeted each other and so forth. You know, like if we met in the street or I saw her up at Pentrillick House. In fact the last time I saw her was the night I was attacked and I said hello to her then. She was waiting at the bus stop which in retrospect seems a little odd because I know she drives because she had a VW Beetle in a lovely shade of green."

"Really!" Hetty wracked her brains to think of a reason why Hazel would have taken the bus if she drove.

"Perhaps she was going to a party or out for a drink," suggested Lottie as though reading her sister's mind, "She wouldn't drive if that were the case."

Hetty nodded. "Could be and she probably caught a bus home as well or took a taxi. There are endless possibilities and I suppose to be honest we still take the bus occasionally even though we both drive. Anyway, on a more cheerful note, have you heard, Gideon, that Brett's offered to pay for the church to be decorated?"

"Het, we've been sworn to secrecy. Remember, Brett wants his largesse kept quiet."

Hetty's hand flew to her mouth. "Whoops."

Gideon chuckled. "Don't worry his secret is safe with me and I knew anyway because Sam told me when he visited me in hospital yesterday and he said to keep quiet."

"Talk of the devil," exclaimed Lottie, as the door opened and Vicar Sam entered the room along with Debbie who carried a tea tray.

"You've another visitor," announced Debbie.

"Sam, good of you to call so soon." Gideon began to rise from his chair. "I didn't hear the doorbell ring."

"That's because he came round the back," said Debbie, as she put down the tray, "and I had the door open to let the sun in."

"Don't get up," insisted Sam, as he gently pushed Gideon back into his chair, "I just came round because I wanted to make sure you were home safely. You're certainly looking well now that you're back in the comfort of your own home."

"Thank you. I feel well too." Gideon placed his feet back on the foot stool.

Debbie handed out mugs of tea. "Please excuse the fact the biscuits are broken but," she said, "but I can assure you they taste just as delicious."

Vicar Sam took two halves of different varieties. "Mother would be very impressed to see that you're using them."

"Are these the ones that you took for choir members?" Hetty asked.

"I've no idea," said Gideon, "Are they, Debbie?"

"No, they're not, these are another lot," Debbie took a biscuit and sat down, "The police took the first box away and so I said they could keep them because Penelope had given me another box by then. I think it rather amused them."

"Mother's biscuits seem to be everywhere," chuckled the vicar.

"We were talking about having the church painted just before you arrived," said Hetty. "Have you anyone in mind to do it?"

Vicar Sam dipped his biscuit in his tea. "I thought Ian would be our best bet."

"What Ian the electrician who is doing the lighting for the play?" Hetty asked.

"That's right but he does decorating as well. He's a good chap and very reliable. Isn't that right, Gideon?"

"Yes, he painted the outside of our house and made a smashing job."

"He'll need a bit of scaffolding," said Hetty, "it wouldn't be safe to paint the top bits on a ladder."

Sam laughed. "Don't worry, that's all in hand. He knows someone with a tower he can borrow."

"What's Ian like?" Lottie asked, "I've seen him on several occasions but never actually met him if you know what I mean."

"Salt of the earth," laughed Sam, "he'd do anything for anyone."

"Has he been in the area long?" Lottie was determined to dig deeper even if the vicar did think highly of the electrician.

"Now I'm not the person to ask that," laughed the vicar, "As you know I'm a relative newcomer myself."

"Same here," said Gideon.

Debbie nodded.

"Hmm, we're a right bunch of Johnny-come-latelys, aren't we?" chuckled Hetty, "Because we've only been here for eighteen months or so."

When Hetty and Lottie left, Hetty caught a glimpse of Marlene watching them through the voile curtains in an upstairs window.

"We're being watched," hissed Hetty, nodding towards the upper storey of the house next door to Gideon and Debbie where the figure quickly backed away.

"Being watched," mused Lottie, as something suddenly occurred to her, "You know what, Het, that might be why someone attempted to murder Hazel. Not being watched so much but more having been seen."

"What on earth are you on about, Lottie?"

"Hazel being at the bus stop means she might have seen the person who attacked Gideon when he left the church. In which case that person would have a motive to silence Hazel to stop her telling the police."

"I think you might be onto something there," conceded Hetty, "but why leave it so long? Gideon was attacked on the Wednesday but Hazel wasn't shot for another five days. So if she was going to report it she would surely have done so by then."

"Yes, of course. Oh well, it's food for thought and something else to add to our list of clues."

"But we don't have a list of clues."

"No, not on paper but we do in our heads."

Chapter Fourteen

On Saturday morning, the family packed up their belongings ready for the journey home for the children were due back at school the following Monday. Emma came up to see them off and Zac promised he'd be back at the end of May during half term week to see the play.

"Can we come back and see the play as well?" Vicki asked, hopefully.

Bill shook his head. "No, because I won't be able to get the time off work. Remember we're going to Scotland for two weeks in August."

"But you and Mum don't need to come with us. We can come with Zac."

"If you were older it would be fine but fifteen is too young." Sandra sounded adamant.

"We'll be sixteen in June," reasoned Kate. In her hand she held the sprig of white heather.

"That's as maybe but apart from age it wouldn't be fair on Grandma and Auntie Hetty," snapped Sandra, "you girls can be a bit of a handful."

"Oh no, we wouldn't mind at all, would we, Het?"

"It's alright with me if it's alright with you," said Hetty, addressing Sandra and Bill, "in fact it'd be nice for the girls to go to the beach and so forth because the weather should be better by then and I'm sure they would behave."

"I think you've forgotten something rather important," Bill reminded them, "you'll both be doing your GCSEs before and after half term so you'll have lots of revision to do."

"Good heavens, yes," exclaimed Sandra, "definitely no then."

Vicki scowled. "But Zac will need to study too for his A Levels and you're letting him come back."

"Zac's promised to study while here and we know he will because he's dedicated."

"Please don't think I'm interfering," said Hetty, "but if the girls are allowed to come here then Lottie and I would make sure they put in the necessary time to revise, wouldn't we, Lottie?"

Lottie saw the look of hope in the eyes of her granddaughters and her heart melted. "Yes, we would and it would be nice to think we were able to help them towards their futures."

"Oh, please say yes," Kate begged. Her fingers gripped the white heather tightly.

Bill looked at Sandra. "What do you think, love?"

"Well, I suppose revising here is as good as anywhere and it might even be better than at home because their friends won't be able to call round here and distract them."

"Good point." He turned to his mother and aunt. "Are you sure you don't mind?"

"Positive," said Lottie. Hetty nodded to confirm her agreement.

"Okay then, yes, but you must promise to behave and revise for at least two hours every day and if I hear anything to the contrary, I'll drive down overnight and take you home. Understood?"

"Understood," shouted Kate and Vicki in unison, as they hugged their parents and then their grandmother and great aunt.

By lunchtime they were ready to leave.

"Drive carefully," said Lottie, "and ring when you get back so we know you're home safely."

"I will, and when we've gone at least you'll have more time to get on with your investigations." Bill chuckled as he sat down on the driver's seat.

"I shall miss your cheek," smiled Hetty.

They drove down Long Lane and then along the main street; as they passed Sea View Cottage they saw Brett packing things into the boot of his car.

"Looks like Brett's going back to London," observed Zac.

"Well, I suppose he has to," reasoned Sandra, "because he won't earn much money down here unless he's spending his time writing."

"I think he spends more time in the pub than anywhere else," laughed Bill. "He's been in there every time I've gone in since Alina went up to London."

On Monday evening, Sid the plumber looked into the mirror at his home in Honeysuckle Close and stroked the moustache he was growing for his role as the detective inspector in the play. For after discussing his appearance with Robert, they had decided that to look the part he ought to have a moustache like Inspector Poirot and a mac like Inspector Clouseau. Sid was feeling proud for the moustache was growing nicely and earlier in the day Daisy, who was doing the costumes along with Lottie, rang to say she had found a suitable mac in the charity shop which should it fit would be ideal. Sid, delighted by the news had gone along to the charity shop during his lunch break to try it on. It was perfect. Feeling that everything was going well, Sid picked up his script and went off to the village hall for a rehearsal quoting his lines with confidence as he strode down the road.

Neither Kitty nor Lottie went to the practice that evening and so when it finished, Hetty bypassed the Crown and Anchor and went straight home. Lottie was in the sitting room watching television when she arrived back and she could tell by the speed at which her sister removed her shoes and coat that she had something of interest to report.

"Well," said Hetty as she sat down on the settee, "Marlene said something tonight which has got me thinking. She suggested that the robbery at Pentrillick House was probably an inside job and was done so they could claim the insurance. That would explain why none of the stolen stuff was ever found. What do you think?"

Lottie scowled. "But isn't that the reason for the robbery in your play?"

"Yes, but there could be something in it and if so maybe Hazel Mitchell knew about it and had to be disposed of."

"Hetty," scolded Lottie, "that's a terrible thing to say. The Liddicott-Treens are lovely people and they would never simulate a robbery to get the insurance and they most certainly wouldn't have tried to murder poor Hazel. This play is blurring your common sense and making you unable to tell fact from fiction."

Hetty looked downcast. "But it sounded so believable when Marlene suggested it."

"Well, I hope the others who were at the practice told her that her theory was silly."

Hetty nodded. They did...all of them."

"Good, and another thing worth bearing in mind is that Hazel has not been working for the Liddicott-Treens long and she certainly wasn't there when the robbery took place. She wasn't even widowed then."

"I wish you'd come to *all* the meetings, Lottie, instead of one here and there. You're more down to earth than me."

"I will, in a few weeks' time when you're practising without scripts as by then costumes will need to be discussed in more detail. I'm looking forward to working with Daisy to sort them out and the charity shop will be a good source for garments."

"Hmm, well you won't have long to wait because Robert said we must all know our lines by the beginning of May and that'll be here before we know it."

Lottie smiled. "Ginny will be busy from May onwards then if she's the prompter."

"She certainly will and I'm sure it'll be a test of her patience."

"Was Brett at the rehearsal tonight?"

"No, he's gone back to London. Someone said he went on Saturday and I've just remembered something else," Hetty's eyes sparkled, "All drama group members and their partners and so forth are invited to Saltwater House for a garden party on Bank Holiday Monday. Isn't that exciting?"

Lottie frowned. "Where on earth is Saltwater House? It's not a name I've come across before."

"Me neither so I asked Tess and I gather it's up that track which runs off the main street shortly after the pub. I've never been up there because it looks like it's private property."

"Which it probably is. So who lives up there?"

"This Paul bloke, you know, the one who's just arrived back on the scene. Apparently he wants to have a little do to thank drama group members for the fun he had a couple of years ago."

"But we weren't members then. We weren't even living down here."

"I know but everyone's invited, old and new."

Chapter Fifteen

On Tuesday evening, Hetty and Lottie walked down to the village hall to play bingo because Hetty said that she was feeling lucky. The weather was fine and as they walked along the main street they saw Marlene ahead standing outside the post office. Before they reached her a red car pulled up on the road and she climbed into the front passenger seat.

"Quick, duck!" commanded Hetty, as she grabbed her sister's arm and pulled her behind a parked van. After the red car had driven by they both stood up.

"Why did you do that?" Lottie asked.

"Because I didn't want her to know we had seen her." Hetty watched as the car disappeared round the bend.

"Why?"

"Why, because she's probably up to no good, that's why."

"By doing what? You really do overreact, Het as I'm sure whatever she's doing is completely innocent."

"No, I doubt it. I bet she's got a fancy man. She looks a flighty piece and she's always fawning around Brett and Robert. I wish I'd been able to get a look at the driver."

They commenced walking towards the village hall.

"Well, the driver wasn't Brett or Robert, that I do know," said Lottie, "because Robert drives a black VW Golf and Brett has a silver BMW and Brett's not here anyway because you said he went back to London on Saturday."

"Well I never," laughed Hetty, "that's not bad considering a year ago you didn't know one make of car from another."

"You're quite right, I didn't, but driving has made me notice cars more than I used to and I'm rather intrigued by all the shapes and sizes."

"Really? So, what was that red car that Marlene went off in?"

"A Ford Fiesta of course."

"Wow, I'm impressed. I wouldn't have had a clue."

"Wouldn't you?"

"No, so you're one up on me there."

When they arrived at the village hall they were surprised to see Debbie Elms standing by a table and in the process of hanging her jacket on the back of a chair.

"Lovely to see you," said Hetty, going straight over to where Debbie stood. "We didn't know you were a bingo fan."

Debbie smiled. "I've been ordered out of the house. Gideon said I need to get out and meet people because I spend too much time at home, bless him. Trouble is, I don't really know many people when it comes to going out alone so I thought I'd try my hand at bingo."

"You've not played before then?"

"No, but I believe it's pretty straightforward."

"Child's play," said Lottie, "come and sit with us. It'll be nice for us to have your company."

In between games, the sisters told Debbie in hushed tones of their efforts to find out who was responsible for the recent crimes.

"Now that sounds right up my street so if you want another opinion please don't hesitate to ask me, after all three heads are better than two."

This prompted Lottie to tell Debbie of Marlene's suspicious behaviour just witnessed.

"And who knows," chuckled Hetty, "she might be involved in all sorts of other dodgy things as well. In fact that's probably why she's good at her part in the play."

"What do you mean?" Lottie asked.

"In the play she's the hairstylist's deceitful, conniving wife and I reckon she's the same in real life."

Debbie tried hard not to laugh. "Well I know we're not her favourite people but I'm pretty sure she wouldn't resort to assault nor do I think she would attempt to steal from the church so I think we can rule her out there."

"We agree but things are always more complicated than they seem on the surface," said Lottie.

"Absolutely, so do you think she might have a fancy man?" Hetty asked.

Debbie smiled broadly. "No idea and she certainly wouldn't tell me if she had."

It was dark when they left the village hall but as they neared the church they spotted the red Fiesta they had seen earlier pull up on the opposite side of the road to the post office. Marlene leaned across and gave the driver a peck on the cheek and then stepped out onto the pavement. She waved as the car tooted and drove away and then turned the corner into St Mary's Way where she and Gary lived.

"See what we mean," said Hetty to Debbie, "Don't you think that's a bit fishy?"

"Yes, I must admit I do."

"But wherever she's been she's not been away long," reasoned Lottie. "Two hours at the most."

"Hmm, probably can't be away any longer or Gary would be suspicious. And at least we know now that the driver of the car was a bloke."

"Perhaps he's her brother," Lottie suggested.

"But if so why pick her up outside the post office and not at her house?"

"I don't know."

Debbie shook her head. "She doesn't have a brother that I do know. Sisters, yes, two in fact, but no brother."

Hetty rubbed her hands with glee. "There you are then. I reckon she's been off with her fancy man having told Gary she was going to bingo."

"But he'd have smelled a rat surely because Marlene never goes to bingo," said Lottie.

"There's a first time for everything, look at Debbie here. Anyway, shall we pop in the pub for a quick drink? My treat since I won twenty pounds."

Lottie nodded. "Yes, I'd like that, Het, because the house seems awfully quiet now the family have gone home."

"How about you. Debbie?"

"Yes please. Sounds like a very good idea. I must admit I do like a drink but Gideon hardly ever touches the stuff."

"You're in good company then," laughed Hetty as they crossed the road and headed towards the Crown and Anchor.

Chapter Sixteen

On Wednesday morning, Hetty and Lottie went for another visit to Pentrillick House because the previous evening while discussing events with Debbie they had decided they ought to try and establish the location of the room in which the valuables stolen had been on display. They knew the room was no longer part of the tour but nevertheless thought its whereabouts might help them try and visualise how the robbery had proceeded. What's more, they were keen to scrutinise the tour guides as both Christopher and the female whose name they couldn't remember were suspects in their eyes for the robbery in 2013 and the attempted murder of Hazel Mitchell on Easter Monday. For although it was Christopher who had found Hazel slumped in the hallway with gunshot wounds it was still possible that he could have shot her through the window from outside and then returned indoors quickly by a side entrance.

Debbie declined the invitation to go snooping with the sisters on the grounds that because Gideon worked at Pentrillick House part-time she thought it unwise in case someone observed her suspicious behaviour, for she knew he was very happy with his job and the people he worked with and she had no wish to jeopardise his position there.

The tour of the house took the same route as when they had been before and so it was obvious that unless their guide, Christopher, mentioned the theft and pointed out the room in question they would be none the wiser and since they knew that to have the room pointed out wasn't part of the tour Hetty took it upon herself to ask.

"Excuse me, Christopher," she said in her sweetest voice, "I heard tell the other day of a robbery here a few years back and that the things stolen were never recovered. Apparently the valuables were in a locked room which was part of the tour. Will we go in there today?"

Christopher actually smiled. "No, and for a very good reason that being as you say the valuables were never recovered and so there is nothing to see but I will point out the room to you when we pass it."

"Oh, thank you, that's very kind."

"Were you working here back then when it happened?" Lottie asked, in an equally sweet voice.

"Yes, and it was a very stressful time. The family were on holiday when the thieves broke in and we felt we'd let them down."

Several other members of the tour expressed interest after that and although Christopher willingly answered their questions, Hetty and Lottie who listened intently learned nothing they had not already heard before. But at least they established the location of the secure room; it was the last one along the hallway, next to the library.

After the tour they walked down to the lake and while there sitting on a bench they saw a man with a bucket of chopped up vegetables which he fed to the swans and ducks.

"Did you see that?" Lottie asked, as she watched the man walk away from the lake.

"Yes, they must have been hungry the way they gobbled that lot down."

"No, no, I wasn't actually thinking along those lines. I was more taken with the bucket, you see, because it suddenly struck me that the bucket would have been the perfect place to hide the gun ready to drop it into the lake."

Hetty sat forward. "You're right. Good thinking, Lottie. So I wonder who he is. I can't say that I've ever seen him before but then I was more taken with the swans and ducks than him so didn't even look at his face."

"I did and I didn't recognise him but he did look vaguely familiar."

"Hmm, we need to find out his identity then."

Lottie laughed. "Well, we know who to ask."

"Yes, Tess. We'll pop into Taffeta's Tea Shoppe on the way home and see if she's working today. I'm sure we could force a cup of coffee down and even a chocolate éclair."

During a brief chat with Tess who waited on their table they learned that the groundsman at Pentrillick House whose job it was to feed the swans and ducks was a man called Ben. And despite the fact Tess said he was gentle, kind, good natured and well thought of, when they got home they added him to their list of suspects.

Over the next few days the weather turned hot and sunny. On Saturday it was glorious and so Hetty and Lottie drove to a garden centre and bought several new plants and then spent an enjoyable afternoon in the garden, planting, weeding and deadheading.

"Shall we plant some of your tomatoes in the flower beds when they're a bit bigger?" Lottie asked, "They would fill a few gaps nicely."

"Yes, good idea because there are far too many for the greenhouse."

"I'll dig over this area here for them and then we'll just have to keep our fingers crossed and hope we have a dry, sunny summer so they don't get blight."

After their chores were done, they sat down on the lawn and soaked up the sun.

Meanwhile, in the garden of Wood Cottage, Lucy Lacey walked amongst the white heather picking fresh, healthy flowers. When her small basket was full, she returned indoors and tipped out the flowers onto the kitchen table. Painstakingly she checked each one for blemishes and trimmed them all to equal lengths; she then tied a piece of cotton to each stem. Once the task was complete she returned them all to the basket and carried them up to the spare bedroom where George was sleeping in a ray of sunlight on a patchwork counterpane made by her mother which covered the spare bed. She reached for a footstool and placed it beneath the beams and from them she took down sprigs already dried and replaced them with the new.

Lucy loved growing a variety of flowers, herbs and vegetables but heather was her passion. Much of her adult life she had spent working as a florist in Plymouth. The shop was owned by an aunt who had offered her a job when she left school knowing that she had a broad knowledge of horticulture and a flair for the wellbeing of flowers. At first she was reluctant to leave her parents but they insisted that she should go and never once had she regretted it.

Sadly the nice weather didn't last and on Sunday morning the inhabitants of Cornwall woke up to grey skies and frequent showers. Nevertheless, Hetty and Lottie went to church despite the rain for they were keen to see if Gideon was well enough to play the organ as Debbie said he might. When they arrived home Lottie promptly switched on the television to watch the London Marathon while Hetty switched on the kettle.

"Humph, typical, it's lovely and sunny up there, Het," Lottie said in a raised voice so that her sister in the kitchen could hear.

"Yes, I heard someone saying after church that this year's marathon will be the hottest day in its twenty whatever-year history."

Lottie sat down. "Poor souls, it's bad enough walking in the heat without having to run in it. Not that we have any heat to walk or run in down here today."

"Have you spotted Luke yet?" Hetty eagerly asked as she entered the sitting room and handed her sister a mug of coffee.

"No, it's a bit like looking for a needle in a haystack."

Hetty sat down. "Any idea if he's dressed in running stuff or if he's a fun-runner?"

"He's a fun-runner," said Lottie, "because if you remember Daisy told us they'd been through the fancy dress stuff in the charity shop to help him out."

"Yes that's right I remember now but I've forgotten what he chose in the end?"

Lottie laughed. "He chose to be a seagull."

"Well, in that case it shouldn't be difficult to spot him."

"No, and with the awkwardness of it I should imagine he'll be quite a way back."

The sisters sat with their eyes transfixed on the television screen determined to see their erstwhile neighbour who was also a member of the drama group.

"I give up," said Lottie after twenty minutes, "it's starting to strain my eyes." She leaned back in her chair.

"Me too and I'm inclined to think we're wasting our time. Shall I switch it off?"

"No, leave it on and we'll just glance at it from time to time."

Hetty unfolded the crumpled pages of her script and started to read through her lines. Lottie picked up the coffee mugs to return them to the kitchen but before she left the room she glanced at the television set just in case Luke was on the screen. What she saw caused her to gasp, "Oh my goodness, look at the television, Hetty, quick." Lottie flapped her mugless hand towards the television set, "There's Brett. Look, look there's Brett on the right hand side of the screen."

Hetty dropped down the script, sprang from her chair and knelt on the floor in front of the television set beside Lottie who had also fallen to her knees. She was just in time to see Brett standing amongst the crowd in the Mall with his arm around an attractive brunette. "You're right, but who is that with him? It's not Alina."

They both tried to look closer but were too late, the coverage had moved back to another leg of the race.

"We might see him again," said Lottie, hopefully."

The sisters watched until the end of the broadcast but saw no further glimpses of Brett with the brunette or of Luke running.

Chapter Seventeen

It was foggy and drizzly on Tuesday evening but that didn't deter Hetty and Lottie from walking down to the village to play bingo again for although neither of them mentioned it both were eager to see if Marlene was picked up in a red Ford Fiesta as during the previous week. To their delight she was there again standing outside the post office beneath an umbrella and looking along the road in an easterly direction. Keen to see if the same car appeared, the sisters slowed their pace and even stopped at one point so that Hetty could pretend to tighten her shoe lace even though her shoes were slip-ons.

"It's coming," whispered Lottie, as Hetty stood back up, "Quick, let's hide again."

As before they hid behind a parked vehicle, this time a car which meant they had to crouch lower. After the red car passed by, they both stood up.

"Damn, we should have looked at the registration number," tutted Hetty.

"Oaf," said Lottie.

"I beg your pardon. Who are you calling an oaf?"

Lottie laughed. "The registration number was OAF. Well, part of it was anyway."

"Oh, I see. Silly me. It's a local car then."

When they arrived at the village hall they were pleased to see that Debbie was already there. She waved as they walked in.

"We hoped you'd be here," whispered Hetty, looking over her shoulder, "We brought our list of suspects to show you on the off-chance."

"How exciting. Shall we go to the pub again afterwards and look at it then?"

Hetty nodded. "That's the plan."

"Lovely, I told Gideon we probably would and he seemed really pleased."

"You've not told him of our sleuthing, have you?" Hetty asked.

Debbie giggled. "No, of course not. Some things are best kept quiet."

"Did you by any chance watch any of the London Marathon?" Lottie asked, as she unbuttoned her coat.

"A bit," admitted Debbie, "I was hoping to see Luke but gave up after a while. Did you watch it?"

"Yes, and we didn't see Luke either but you'll never guess who we did see."

Debbie shook her head. "No idea. Who?"

"Brett," blurted Hetty, "He was amongst the crowd of spectators in the Mall with a striking brunette and had his arm around her."

"Are you sure? I mean, sure it was him?"

"Definitely," said Hetty, "we got a real good look at him but sadly the cameramen didn't give us a second glimpse which is a shame because we really wanted to scrutinise the woman he was with."

"Not that we would have known her," reasoned Lottie.

"No, we wouldn't unless she was famous," Hetty conceded.

"Well, I suppose these things happen with showbiz type people," tutted Debbie, dismissively, "and it doesn't have any bearing on the goings-on down here, does it?"

"No," admitted Hetty, "I suppose not but it's interesting nevertheless."

"And slightly tarnishes his reputation in my eyes," Lottie added.

The three ladies eagerly left the village hall at exactly the same time as the previous week hoping for a repeat performance of Marlene returning to the village. To their dismay there was no sighting of the red car anywhere between the village hall and the Crown and Anchor even though they walked at a very slow pace.

"How disappointing," Hetty grumbled, "Still, never mind, we'll try again next week."

After they had arrived at the Crown and Anchor and bought their drinks, they saw Tess by the piano along with her husband. When she saw the sisters and Debbie she waved and walked over to speak to them. "Have you learned your lines yet?" she asked Hetty.

"I'm getting there, how about you?"

"Same for me but with so much going on I can't seem to concentrate for long."

"That's understandable," said Lottie, sympathetically, "and you work as well so you don't have a great deal of free time."

Hetty laughed. "Sadly I don't have that excuse as I have all the time in the world."

"So is there any more news about the recent crimes?" Lottie asked before Hetty had the chance.

Tess wrinkled her nose. "Not really although I've heard on the grapevine that Hazel was seeing a chap who her two children didn't approve of. Apparently he's a real charmer and a bit of a playboy."

"Hazel with a playboy! Surely not." Lottie was shocked.

"Well, that's what I've heard," Tess chuckled, "I even know his name."

"We're all ears," Hetty moved closer.

"He's called Andrew Banks and he lives in Helston somewhere near the boating lake. I don't know exactly where but it's quite near to one of her children and so for that reason whenever she goes to see him she never drives in case her son spots her car as it's quite a conspicuous colour."

"Ah, so that's why she was at the bus stop on the night that Gideon was attacked," tutted Lottie, "she was going to meet this Andrew Banks."

Tess nodded. "Precisely."

"Where on earth do you get these facts from?" Hetty was intrigued.

"All sorts of places but in this case from Cynthia who lives two doors away from me. She's a tour guide up at the house as well as Christopher and she and Hazel are good friends."

"Hmm, interesting," Hetty mused, "I think we'll have to investigate further. Thank you, Tess. What would we do without you?"

"It's my pleasure. As you know I do like a bit of gossip and I think the people I share it with do to." She winked mischievously and then returned to her husband.

"Cynthia," whispered Hetty, "that's the name we couldn't remember the other day." She took several gulps of wine. "We'll find a table and then I'll add her to our suspect list before I forget again."

"So is Cynthia a tour guide at Pentrillick House?" Debbie asked.

"Yes, and she has a very annoying voice," hissed Hetty.

They found a quiet corner and sat down and Hetty added Cynthia to the list. She then passed the sheet of paper to Debbie for her perusal.

"Well, I'm pleased to see that you didn't include me in your list."

Hetty laughed. "Hmm, we slipped up there, Lottie, because usually people we don't know very well become prime suspects."

"Quite right because it could easily be me," suggested Debbie, her tone of voice earnest, "I mean, I could have been there waiting and attacked Gideon when he came into the vestry. My motive being he was having an affair with Hazel who he met while working at Pentrillick House. That would also give me a motive for shooting Hazel, wouldn't it?"

Hetty's jaw dropped. Lottie's heart rate increased.

Debbie laughed. "Don't look at me like that. I'm just trying to demonstrate that no-one should be ruled out. Not even me."

"Ah, but I would have ruled you out early," Hetty grinned with satisfaction, "and for one obvious reason."

"And what's that?"

"The fact Gideon would have recognised the ringtone if it were your phone left on the vestry floor."

"And if it was you that attacked him you would have just hit him without bothering to go through the chest," Lottie added, "and you certainly wouldn't have taken the candlesticks from the altar."

"I might have," smiled Debbie, mischievously, "if I wanted it to look like attempted robbery, but yes, I agree you've come up with some good reasons but you can see the point I was trying to make, can't you?"

"Yes, we can," agreed Hetty, "and so I think it's very likely the person we're looking for *is* actually on our list."

"Or isn't," said Lottie, thoughtfully, "because it's possible he or she could be someone we know, really like and would never consider, hence they're not on the list."

Hetty laughed. "In which case everyone in the village is a suspect."

"On the other hand," said Debbie, "it could be someone that none of us have ever clapped eyes on before."

"That's a dreadful thought," cried Hetty, "because if he's someone we don't know then how on earth are we ever going to find him?"

It was eleven o'clock when they left the Crown and Anchor. The rain had stopped and as they waited by the kerb to cross the road into Long Lane a car drove by.

"The red Fiesta," gasped Hetty, watching as the car drove through a puddle further along the street.

Quickly the three ladies crossed the road where they were just able to see the Fiesta pull up as before opposite the post office. None of them were surprised to see Marlene step from the car and wave as it drove away.

"That was a much longer night out," gabbled Hetty, "We need to look into this and see what she's up to."

"Meanwhile, I'll follow her to St Mary's Avenue and see if she goes straight home," said Debbie.

"Good thinking," agreed Lottie, "Off you go because she has quite a head start."

"Right, goodnight and I'll be in touch tomorrow."

On Thursday afternoon, Hetty and Lottie decided to take a walk to the address where Hazel Mitchell lived because the day before, their next door neighbour, Chloe, told them that she had heard how touched Hazel's son and daughter were by the amount of get well cards that had been posted through their mother's letterbox. On hearing this Hetty subtly asked Chloe where Hazel lived so they might also send a card, although the real reason was that she hoped while there delivering it, they might see someone of interest, namely Andrew Banks. Debbie went with the sisters and as luck would have it there was a small garden park opposite Hazel's house and a bench faced her front door. Delighted that they'd be able to sit and watch without looking suspicious, the three ladies sat down and waited.

"Of course, it'd help if we had some idea of what he looked like," said Lottie.

"I agree, and I suppose in reality if her son and daughter disapprove of him he's not likely to leave a card here anyway."

"Or he might already have done so if he was close to Hazel," reasoned Debbie.

"Hmm, yes of course, and if he did I wonder if they passed it on to her." Hetty frowned as she thought.

"There wouldn't be much point at this stage, would there, Het? Remember poor Hazel is in a coma so she won't be able to look at anything."

"Good point," said Hetty, "but we'll hang around for a while just on the off-chance."

During the first half hour they were there only one person put anything through Hazel's letterbox and that was the postman. Shortly afterwards a white van pulled up and its driver took a parcel from the back but that was delivered to the house next door.

"Oh dear, I think we're wasting our time," admitted Hetty, "Shall we go home?"

But before Lottie or Debbie had a chance to answer a car pulled up in front of Hazel's gate and a young man stepped out.

"Well, I never. You know who that is, don't you?" Lottie asked.

Both Debbie and Hetty shook their heads.

"It's the chap who feeds the ducks and swans at Pentrillick House. Ben I think Tess said his name is."

"Oh, is it really?" Debbie asked, "I've heard Gideon mention him. I think they get on quite well because they have a lot in common and if I remember correctly Ben is in the church choir."

"Of course," gushed Lottie, realising why he had looked vaguely familiar, "hardly a hardened criminal then."

"That's interesting, Debbie," mused Hetty, ignoring her sister, "so I wonder why he's come up here?"

Lottie frowned. "Well, that's obvious. He works at Pentrillick House and so no doubt Hazel knows him the same as Gideon does."

Instead of going home by the quickest route the three ladies decided to walk around some of the back streets which were unfamiliar to them. After crossing a few roads and turning corners they came across a recreation field opposite a row of semi-detached, pebble-dashed houses.

"These must be council houses," surmised Debbie, noting they were all the same style.

"Or were," agreed Hetty, "it looks like several have been bought judging by the different style doors and various upgrades."

Lottie read the name on a metal plate attached to the garden wall of the first house. "We're in Hawthorn Road. I like that name; it's a bit like Blackberry Way."

"Only in as much as they both have thorns and grow in hedges," laughed Hetty.

"Yes, I suppose you're right." Lottie cast her eyes along the row of houses. "If I remember correctly we were told that someone we've recently come across lives up here but I can't recollect who. Can you, Het?"

"It does sound familiar I must admit but no I can't remember either."

As they strolled along the pavement they caught sight of someone trimming a hedge in the last house.

"Pickle," said Lottie, nodded towards the figure, "it's Pickle who lives up here and that's him."

Hetty squinted. "Are you sure?"

"Positive, you'll be able to see when we get nearer."

"Who is Pickle?" Debbie asked, "I've never heard mention of that name before."

"He's a poacher," sighed Hetty, "and his name is Percy Pickering but everyone calls him Pickle because as a boy he couldn't say Pickering so called himself Pickle. That's probably not quite right but it's near enough."

"Oh, I see. I think that's rather charming."

As they got nearer they saw it was the poacher and to their surprise he greeted them warmly and wished them a good day.

"And good day to you too. This is a lovely spot. Very tranquil." Hetty was keen to learn anything she could about the poacher.

"Yes, I love it up here. It's well away from the main street and the air feels fresher."

"So have you been here long?" Lottie asked.

Pickle hooked the shears over the garden gate, took a tissue from his pocket and wiped his forehead. "Yes, I've been in this same house since I got married and we were lucky enough to buy it in the early nineties. Both our boys were born here but they've flown the nest now so I'm all on my own as my dear wife died a few years back."

"Oh, I'm sorry to hear that," sympathised Lottie, "Have your sons gone far?" She knew she had been told where but couldn't remember.

"One's in Taunton, the other Falmouth so he's quite near."

Remembering Pickle did gardening jobs, Hetty peeped over the gate where neatly trimmed lawns on either side of a central path were surrounded by borders crammed with colourful spring flowers. "It looks like you enjoy your garden, Mr Pickering. It's very pretty."

"Thank you, I do, but please call me Pickle. Everyone else does."

"I'm fond of gardening," said Debbie, "it's good exercise and productive too."

Pickle picked up the shears. "I won't disagree with you there. I'd rather be in my garden any day than be in crowds."

"You're not one for the shops then?" Hetty asked.

"No, and thank goodness for the internet. That's where I do my shopping. I even have my groceries delivered so I don't have to bother traipsing around the supermarket."

"He seems a really nice chap," stated Lottie as they continued on their way and were out of earshot.

"You can't judge a book by its cover," Hetty scoffed.

"Well, in my opinion anyone who likes gardening is alright," Debbie said.

"Hmm, but in my opinion anyone who does a bit of poaching is dishonest and so I shall keep an open mind about Mr Pickering."

Chapter Eighteen

"How unusual," said Lottie, on Saturday morning, as she pulled back the sitting room curtains and looked up at the clear blue sky, "Bank Holidays are usually wet. I do hope this nice spell of weather lasts until Monday for the do at Saltwater House."

"It's supposed to," remarked Hetty, "I must admit I'm looking forward to the garden party if for no other reason than to see the house. I reckon being near to the sea it should have lovely views."

The good weather did last and on Bank Holiday Monday afternoon the sisters left Primrose Cottage and walked down to the village. They had briefly considered taking Albert but decided it would be unfair to Paul; the house was not his and so he would be responsible for any damage during his occupation. Not that Albert would do any serious damage to the property but he was prone to digging holes in the garden.

The dirt track which led to Saltwater House was a short distance past the Crown and Anchor on the left-hand side of the road. Wild primroses, violets and bluebells grew in profusion on the grass verges and above, hawthorn, elder and the white blossom of blackthorn flourished amongst twisted brambles. The gate at the end of the track was wide open; a welcoming gesture for visitors who chose to arrive by car.

Once through the gate the sisters followed a gravel path which wound its way through shrubs and an array of small fir trees. At the end of the path was the house, large, detached and painted white, dazzling to the eye in the bright afternoon sunshine.

Several group members were already there and seated on extensive lawns beyond which lay a breath-taking view of the sea.

"Must be costing a fortune to rent this place if he's here for the summer," whispered Hetty to Ginny, having thanked their host for his kind invitation and poured themselves drinks from the vast selection of bottles on a makeshift bar.

"I think he knows the people that own it," divulged Ginny, "They're away on a cruise so appreciate having someone here to keep an eye on things. That's what I heard anyway."

"So who does own it?" Lottie asked.

"I only know the name and it's Goldsworthy. I've never met or even seen them. In fact I don't even know how many of them there are, but then they only bought the place a couple of months ago."

"Six months ago actually and there are two of them. A man and a woman but I don't know their relationship or their ages." Alex waved his arm at two empty chairs, "Aren't you two going to sit down?"

"Thank you, yes," The sisters each took a seat.

"Isn't Goldsworthy a Cornish name?" Lottie asked, as she placed her glass of white wine on the table.

"I believe so," said Ginny, "but I'm not sure why I think that."

The other guests arrived in dribs and drabs. One of the last was Vicar Sam who carried a box of broken biscuits beneath his arm. He handed them to Daisy and Maisie. "The last box," he said, "Mother asked me to give them to you and I've been meaning to drop them off at the charity shop for some time but I've always managed to forget."

"Oh, lovely," cried Maisie, looking at the picture of biscuits on the side of the box, "we shall enjoy them with our tea breaks."

As Maisie tucked the box beneath the table, Debbie, and Gideon who had recently joined the drama group to help Kitty with the music and the piano accompaniment for dramatic effect, appeared along the gravel path.

"Over here," Lottie beckoned to the latest arrivals when she spotted them walking away from the bar with drinks in hand.

"I've persuaded Gideon to have a gin and tonic," smiled Debbie, as they took seats round the table with Hetty, Lottie, Ginny and Alex.

"More like tonic and gin," laughed Gideon, "it's very weak and I must admit it's actually quite nice. Refreshing too, especially on a glorious day like this."

"I take it you're not too fond of alcohol then?" Alex commented.

Gideon shook his head. "No, I'm not, I don't know why but it's just never appealed to me. Debbie likes a drink though, don't you, love?"

Debbie nodded eagerly.

"Well, each to their own," declared Ginny, conscious of her brim-full glass of chardonnay, "but I think the world would be far less rosy without wine."

On a bench beneath a cherry tree in full blossom, sat Brett and Alina; close by was a picnic table around which sat Kitty, Tommy, Tess, and hairdressers, Karen and Nicki.

"Couldn't your husband make it?" Kitty asked Tess.

"No, sadly not, he's working but he sends his regards to you all."

"Nice to see you both back," said Kitty to Brett and Alina, "have you finished filming now, Alina?"

"Yes, well, no. That is to say, I've finished all I have to do but there's still lots more to be filmed that doesn't involve me."

"I see, well, you've certainly picked a lovely weekend to be back."

Hetty's ears pricked up. "Although I suppose it's even warmer in London," she said, knowing full well that it was, "We watched the marathon the other day hoping to see Luke and it was very hot for that. Did you watch it while you were up there?"

"No, I'm not really into that sort of thing," claimed Brett, shaking his head, "Looks too much like hard work."

"Me neither," agreed Alina, "although I did see snippets of it on the News."

"It must have been hell running in that heat," said Bernie, "I don't know how Luke did it."

"Is Luke coming here this afternoon?" Alina asked.

"No, he and Natalie have gone up to visit his parents for the Bank Holiday," answered Tess.

"So out of interest, did he do all twenty six miles?" Brett asked.

"Yes and he wore his medal at the play practice the following day." Robert took out his phone and showed Brett and Alina a picture he'd taken at the rehearsal of Luke and his medal.

Sid arrived late because he had been called out to mend a leaking pipe. After he was greeted by everyone, Maisie beckoned him over to where she sat with Daisy and their respective husbands.

"I've something for you," Maisie reached beneath the table, "I found it in the back of the stockroom yesterday."

She handed him a large carrier bag and from it Sid took a trilby hat.

"Wow brilliant," he laughed, as he placed it on his head, "How does it look?"

"Very dapper," exclaimed Robert, approvingly, "Well done, Maisie, now Sid's outfit is complete."

"Any luck with my sergeant's uniform?" Vicar Sam asked as he poured Guinness from a can into a glass.

"We think we'll have to hire one," said Robert, "but that's not a problem. I know a firm who provide an excellent service. Just jot down your measurements some time and I'll give them a ring."

"If this lovely weather continues," yawned Ginny, leaning back to feel the warmth of the sun on her face, "we'll be wishing we could do our performances at the Minack Theatre."

Alex laughed. "I know we're good but we're not that good."

"I don't know," chuckled Robert, "Some of you are very polished but I think we're more suited to the village hall."

"Well, at least we're guaranteed an audience when it's in the village," said Sid, "because the locals like to come and see us make fools of ourselves."

Paul mingled with the guests, chatting to them all in turn and telling them to help themselves to drinks at the bar and food laid out in the kitchen.

"Would it be alright of we had a look round the garden?" Hetty asked, "I'm intrigued to know what's on the other side of that huge hedge."

Paul waved his hand. "Please help yourself. I'm sure you'll not be disappointed."

Hetty stood up. "Thank you."

A grass path twisted and turned through spring flowers in deep attractive borders. The scent of lilac filled the air and a huge magnolia in full flower stood beside a drystone wall. At the end of the path a fountain sprinkled fine water into a small ornamental pond. Beyond the pond the garden began to slope downhill and opened up into an area where plants and small shrubs lay nestled amongst the rocks that led down to the edge of the cliffs.

As Hetty and Lottie returned to the party, Gideon went into the house in search of the bathroom. When asked, Gary, at Seawater House with his wife Marlene, pointed Gideon in the right direction. When he returned to the party outside he seemed rather vague.

"Are you alright?" Debbie asked, "You're frowning."

"Am I? Sorry."

"Yes, why?"

"I've just been to the bathroom and there's an air freshener thing in there and it's triggered off a memory of the night I was attacked."

Everyone stopped talking and looked in Gideon's direction.

"And?" Debbie urged.

"I can't name it but I'm pretty sure it's the same fragrance that I smelled before I got hit on the head."

There were several gasps, cries and wows as nearly everyone made a beeline for the bathroom and sniffed simultaneously.

"Musk," said Karen, "sweetly scented musk. It's rather pleasant."

All agreed.

"You must tell the police," insisted Debbie, "it might help with their enquiries."

Gideon nodded. "Okay, I will when we get home."

"Hmm, we're getting somewhere at last," whispered Hetty to Lottie. "All we need now is to sniff out someone wearing either musk aftershave or perfume and we'll have our culprit."

"An impossible task," scoffed Lottie, "because whoever wore it on the night of Gideon's attack is unlikely to ever wear it again and especially after today's findings get to be common knowledge."

"Then we must make sure that word doesn't get out."

Lottie laughed. "Tess is here, Het. It'll be all round the village before nightfall."

As the afternoon wore on so the drinks flowed and as the sun set over the sea, Debbie was suddenly aware that Gideon was slurring his words.

"Gideon, you're drunk," she squealed in alarm.

"I'm not," he replied, his face set in a silly grin.

Several people were amused; some laughed but Debbie was concerned. "How can anyone get drunk on tonic water with no more than a teaspoon of gin?"

Tess stepped forward and took a sip of Gideon's drink. "I reckon this is near enough neat gin. What do you think, Nicki? You're the gin drinker."

Nicki took a sip and then licked her lips. "Oh goodness me, yes. Not much tonic in that. Who poured Gideon's drink?"

"I did," said Debbie, "that's how I know the balance between the gin and the tonic. Gideon's not been anywhere near the bar."

"Then someone has been having a bit of fun," giggled Nicki, "and they've tried to get your husband drunk."

"Tried," shrieked Debbie, "I think that's an understatement."

All eyes turned to Sid who held up his hands. "Don't look at me. I'm one hundred percent innocent."

"Me too," stated Bernie, as eyes turned towards him.

Debbie giggled as Gideon laid his head on her lap and snored gently. "Can someone help me make him more comfortable, please?"

"We'll take him indoors," said Paul, "and lay him on the couch."

Brett who had watched the ensuing drama with an amused smile on his face suddenly laughed out loud. "I am so glad I bought a cottage in Pentrillick because you lot will definitely inspire my writing."

On Tuesday, Hetty and Lottie decided to go into Helston for Flora Day despite the fact that the morning was cloudy and damp. They rang Debbie to see if she would like to join them but she declined the invitation because she had a dental appointment in Penzance to have a tooth removed. Gideon was due to have gone with his wife so they could do some shopping while in town but he decided against it because he had a thumping headache.

The sisters elected to take the bus into Helston to avoid finding a parking space on what they knew to be a very busy day with several roads closed to traffic. As they approached the bus stop outside the church they found a small crowd already waiting and the bus was on time. Once in Helston they headed towards Meneage Street just in time to watch the children's dance.

"I've never seen so many children in one go," said Hetty, as a long procession of boys and girls aged from young primary to sixth form college and all dressed in white danced along the street behind the town band.

As she spoke a few umbrellas went up in the crowd around them.

"Poor little mites," tutted Lottie, noting the children continued to smile despite the drizzle, "Why couldn't it have been lovely like yesterday?"

However, later in the day after the Midday dance during which the sisters admired the ladies' long dresses and extravagant hats, the weather improved and the sun came out.

"What shall we do now?" Lottie asked, as they walked down the middle of the closed off road.

"Try and find where Andrew Banks lives," replied Hetty, "after all that's one of the reasons why we came here today."

As they walked down towards the boating lake, glancing at the stalls that lined the sides of the streets, Lottie repeatedly sniffed the air.

"Why are you sniffing?" Hetty asked, "Do you have a cold?"

"No, I'm on the lookout for the smell of sweetly scented musk."

Hetty laughed. "Well, the best of luck with that. All I can smell is burgers, sausages, chips and so forth and it's making me feel hungry."

"Me too so shall we get something to eat then?"

"I'm game if you are."

With trays of fish and chips in their hands they climbed over the low wall which ran between the road and the boating lake and sat down on a bench overlooking the water.

"With any luck we'll see Hazel's son while we're here," declared Hetty optimistically as she took from her pocket a picture of the man in question cut out from the local newspaper which had featured an article about his mother's attack.

Lottie looked at the crumpled piece of paper laid out on Hetty's lap. "It's not a very good picture though, is it? And being in black and white it doesn't even tell us what colour his hair is."

"No, but he has quite distinct features so I'm sure I'd recognise him."

Lottie laughed. "Okay but I think the chances of seeing him are zilch."

"But we have to try," hissed Hetty, "and so after lunch we'll walk slowly along the road so as not to miss anything and we'll make a point of looking over garden walls because he might be cutting the grass or something like that."

"What, on Flora Day when there are people everywhere? I think that's highly unlikely, Het. Besides if we did see him how would it help?"

Hetty sighed deeply. "Because it would give us some idea of where Andrew Banks lives."

"Yes, of course, I'd forgotten that." Lottie glanced over to the road and the houses beyond the stalls. "It's not going to be easy though, is it? I mean there are houses everywhere and lots of them are behind the ones along the main road."

"Pessimist," chuntered Hetty.

"No, I'm not really, Het, I'm just being realistic and this seems a bit of a wild goose chase. I think it would be a better idea to try and get an address or something like that for either Hazel's son or better still Andrew Banks and then we'd definitely know where they live."

Hetty looked downcast. "You're right and we don't even know whether they live in houses or bungalows."

"Perhaps we could look in the telephone directory when we get home. That'd give us Andrew's address then it wouldn't matter where Hazel's son lives."

"Providing he's in it. I mean he could be ex-directory or even like so many these days he might not have a landline."

"True." Hetty stood up, walked to a nearby bin and dropped the fish and chips tray inside. "Have you nearly finished because I'm eager to move on now?"

"Yes, I've eaten as much as I can." Lottie threw her remaining chips to four seagulls lurking near to the bin.

"Isn't that illegal?" Hetty asked.

"Isn't what illegal?"

"Feeding seagulls."

"Is it?"

"Yes, I think so. At least it is in some areas because I remember reading about it but I'm not sure whether it was here or somewhere else."

Lottie looked as the gulls noisily finished off the chips. "Quick, let's get lost in the crowd in case anyone saw me."

Hastily they made their exit but after a few yards, Lottie stopped abruptly.

Hetty frowned. "What's the matter, Lottie? Oh my goodness, are we being followed by the police?"

Lottie shook her head. "No, but look over there in that driveway." She pointed in the direction of her fixed gaze.

Hetty gasped. A red Ford Fiesta was parked beneath an apple tree in full blossom and part of its registration number was OAF.

In the gardens of Saltwater House, Paul was busy clearing up after the garden party the previous day. He carried trays of glasses into the house and carefully loaded them into the dishwasher and then returned outdoors to put the garden furniture in its normal position; the spare chairs he put back in the garage. Looking around he saw there was no litter and what little food had been dropped had been cleared up by passing seagulls.

Paul was an accountant and his clients were all wealthy businessmen and women. The reason he was in Cornwall was because his sister and her husband had recently bought Saltwater House and they wanted someone they knew to keep an eye on it while they were away on a world cruise. Paul had happily volunteered. He loved Pentrillick and the location of the house was bought on his recommendation when his sister expressed the desire to have a country retreat near to the sea.

Because of the nature of his work Paul was able to work from home or wherever else he chose to be and that was the reason he was in Cornwall in 2016. In the depths of winter he had felt a sudden desire to spend the coming summer by the sea. He could have bought a house but decided to rent instead. His choice was limited though as most properties already had bookings for the summer months. In the end he settled for a modest house and paid the owner a good price for the six months from the beginning of April until the end of September. It was in the Crown and Anchor shortly after his arrival that he had met Robert Stephens who told him they were always on the lookout for men to take on roles with the village's amateur drama group. Paul had expressed interest and to Robert's delight he agreed to take on the leading role which they had been unable to fill and which Robert feared he might have to fulfil himself.

When the outside was all neat and tidy Paul returned indoors, made himself a coffee and switched on his laptop to check his emails before he started work on the accounts of his clients. No-one in Cornwall knew the nature of Paul's work and because several of his clients were household names he chose to keep it that way. He knew there were several theories doing the rounds and was amused by some of the most obscure.

Most of the emails in his inbox he deleted but one in particular he read with mixed feelings. It was from his ex-wife from whom he had parted amicably three years before. She was due to re-marry in September and was keen for him to attend a large dinner party she was throwing at the weekend so that he might meet her intended. Paul replied promptly saying that he would not be able to make it but wished her and her fiancé all the very best for the future but he did not tell her that he was in Cornwall. As he pressed 'send' he heard a knock on the back door and then it opened.

"Only me, Paul," called a voice, "just wanted to let you know I was here in case you thought someone was lurking in the bushes."

Paul laughed as he went into the kitchen. "Good morning, Pickle. Have you come to plant the roses?"

"I have. They arrived this morning so I thought today would be ideal since it's a bit cloudy."

"I hope you know where they're to go because I don't?"

"Yes, I do. Mrs Goldsworthy and me had a chat before they went away."

"Excellent and you'll be pleased to know members of the drama group were here yesterday and they were very impressed with the gardens."

"That's good but I can only take credit for the maintenance; it was the chap who owned the house before your sister and her husband bought it who did the planning. Before him it was a wilderness apparently."

"So I've heard. Coffee before you go out?"

"Yes please."

"Sit down then." Paul prepared the coffee machine and switched it on.

"So are you going to be in this year's play?" Pickle asked.

Paul shook his head. "No, I've more than enough to keep me occupied and they don't need me anyway because all the parts are taken."

"Any idea what it's about?"

"A murder mystery called *Murder at Mulberry Hall*."

"Hmm, that sounds a bit close to home."

"How do you mean?"

"Hazel Mitchell. Someone tried to kill her up at Pentrillick House. Poor woman. I hope she pulls through."

"You know her then?"

"Yes, I've been doing her garden since her husband died. She's a nice woman."

"Really. So do you have any inclination as to who might have wanted her dead?"

"No, wish I had. Funny thing is though she acted a bit strange when I was last there and when I went into the kitchen to collect my money she was sitting at the table and frowning at something on her laptop. The door was wide open so I knocked and peeped in. She jumped when she saw me and quickly closed down the laptop lid so that I couldn't see what was on the screen."

Paul smiled. "So you didn't get a chance to see anything at all?"

"No, no but I did glimpse one word and that was banks."

Chapter Nineteen

On Tuesday evening, Hetty and Lottie hurried along to bingo eager to tell Debbie of their findings that morning in Helston and as usual they saw Marlene picked up in the red Ford Fiesta outside the post office. However, to their dismay, Debbie did not put in an appearance nor did they see Marlene dropped off as they left the village hall. After a brief discussion they concluded the reason for Debbie's absence was probably due to her tooth extraction and no doubt poor Gideon was still feeling a little under the weather. Because there was no Debbie they decided to give the Crown and Anchor a miss and went straight home.

On Wednesday morning the sisters further discussed the Flora Day findings, hoping that having slept on the subject they might see things more clearly. For having seen the red Fiesta down near the boating lake they had every reason to assume, that Marlene, like Hazel, was an associate of Andrew Banks although try as they might neither could see any possible reason for him to be involved in either of the Pentrillick crimes even though he was an associate of Hazel Mitchell. Because Debbie had not been at bingo, Lottie rang her after breakfast to bring her up to date and see if she agreed with their surmise as regards Andrew Banks. After a brief discussion, Debbie and Lottie conceded they were possibly barking up the wrong tree. For the most probable theory regarding Hazel was that whoever attempted to kill her did so because she saw him leave the church after the attack on Gideon and Gideon was attacked because he disturbed a robbery.

"But who would sink so low as to rob a church anyway?" Lottie asked, after she had relayed the phone conversation with Debbie to her sister.

"Goodness knows. And why would someone go after a silver communion chalice? It'd be worthless unless he knew someone who'd take it off his hands."

"Maybe he was a professional. You know, like the lot that broke into Pentrillick House. Might even be one of the same gang."

"Surely not. The attempted robbery of the church wasn't at all well planned. The muppet didn't even know where the chalice was kept."

"And he probably took the candlesticks rather than leave emptyhanded."

"And hit Gideon over the head with one of them before he made his escape."

"If that's what he was hit with."

"Good point. We don't even know that and it's highly unlikely that the police will tell us but it seems logical to me."

"Which reminds me. Did Gideon tell the police he's identified the mysterious scent as musk?" Hetty asked.

"Yes, but not until this morning. Debbie said they both forgot all about it yesterday."

"Hardly surprising," Hetty smiled as she recalled the events on Monday, "Gideon must have felt dreadful all day."

"He did," confirmed Lottie, "and he vows never to drink again."

Hetty laughed. "I've said that several times myself over the years."

"Yes, I'm sure you have." Lottie looked to the mantelpiece where Hetty's sprig of heather lay. "I know you liked her and we dismissed her when we first created our list of suspects but do you think Lucy Lacey may be involved in any of the crimes? I ask because it's just occurred to me that she lives very near to

Pentrillick House and so would have been able to leave the grounds by way of the woods and avoid being detained by the police."

Hetty's jaw dropped. "Are you suggesting she shot Hazel?"

"Well, um, yes, I suppose I am. I mean, it's feasible that after she had done so she nipped down to the lake tossed the gun into the water and then slipped off into the woods. She would have been on her own and so no-one would have missed her."

Hetty was flabbergasted. "But what could be her motive? She certainly wouldn't have been the person who attempted to steal things from the church."

"I don't know. I really don't know, but she does claim to see things before they happen so perhaps she needed to silence Hazel before she spoke about something she'd seen through her mystic powers."

"But you scoffed at the notion of her having mystic powers," Hetty reminded her sister.

"Well, maybe I was wrong."

Hetty shook her head. "No, I don't think Lucy's in any way involved. What's more, I'm sure had she been at Pentrillick House she would have been seen by someone: after all her outfits are a little eccentric."

Lottie frowned. "But are they? When she called here selling heather the weather was really cold and miserable so she was obviously wrapped up. And when the girls saw her in her cottage she was wearing a spotted dress, cardigan and slippers so nothing unusual there."

Hetty tried hard to come up with reasons to defend Lucy but couldn't.

"Okay, I'll add her to the list if it makes you happy but I think it's very silly."

Lottie smiled. "Yes, it probably is but then so are all the other names on it."

"Except one," reasoned Hetty, "one of them might well be right."

"Or two," Lottie added.

Later that evening, at her home in St Mary's Avenue, Debbie went out into the back garden to bring in the washing. As she unpegged the last item she heard the back door of the adjoining house open and then close followed by light footsteps hurrying down the garden path. Eager to see if she could fathom out who was in such a hurry, Debbie stood perfectly still and listened.

"Hi, Andrew, it's Marlene," she heard her next door neighbour say, "I'm ringing to see if you booked the room okay."

Debbie gasped and tiptoed closer to the fence. All was quiet and so she assumed Marlene was listening to what the person called Andrew was saying.

"You have. Brilliant."

More silence.

"That's wonderful. Anyway, I'd better go. Gary's in the shower but he never takes long."

Another pause.

"Yeah, okay. See you soon. Bye."

Footsteps retreated up the path and when Debbie heard the back door open and then close she picked up the laundry basket and dashed indoors where Gideon was putting on his shoes ready to go to choir practice. She tried to act as normal as possible by folding the washing and putting it in a neat pile on the table.

"Shouldn't be late," said Gideon, as he stood up and pecked her on the cheek.

"Okay, see you later."

When Debbie heard the front door close she dashed into the hallway and rang the ladies at Primrose Cottage.

On Thursday morning, Gideon went to Pentrillick House to work in the gardens until lunchtime. It was his first day back since his attack and he was keen to get active again for he was very conscious of the fact he'd put on a few pounds during his convalescence; a situation not helped by Penelope Prendergast's box of broken biscuits. He was also in a good frame of mind because Debbie told him that while he was away she proposed to visit Hetty and Lottie for a cup of coffee. This pleased him enormously; Debbie was a shy woman and it was good to see she that was making friends and getting out of the house.

When Debbie arrived at Primrose Cottage she found the sisters ready and waiting; list of suspects on the sitting room table and biscuits on a plate.

"I'll make the coffee," insisted Lottie, as Debbie took a seat, "but don't start without me. Talk about the weather or something."

Hetty sat down opposite Debbie. "Lovely day again."

"Yes, it's warm work walking up Long Lane in this heat."

"Mustn't grumble though because we know when it does start to rain it'll never stop."

"Very true. The scent of the lilac in your front garden is gorgeous. I could smell it before I even got to the gate."

"Yes, and for that reason I took several cuttings from it last year. They've all rooted so if you'd like one you're more than welcome."

"That would be fantastic, thank you. I love lilac because it reminds me of when I was young."

Lottie called from the kitchen. "Coming now, so pull out a chair for me."

"Thank goodness," laughed Hetty, as she did as her sister asked, "I'm itching to get on with things."

"Right," said Debbie, once Lottie was seated and they all had mugs of coffee, "have you found anything out?"

"Yes and no," stated Hetty, "but first can you tell us all you know about Marlene and Gary?"

Debbie wrinkled her nose. "Well, there's not a great deal to tell because I've never had much to do with them. I know Marlene works at the village school as a dinner lady and they have two teenage children but then you probably know that anyway."

Hetty nodded. "Yes, we do. How about Gary?"

"Gideon chatted with him when we first moved in because they both come from Lancashire so they talked a bit about places they both knew when they were kids. To be honest we never really see much of them. They don't go to church and we don't go to the pub or at least Gideon doesn't. I've been once or twice now thanks to you two."

"We believe Gary was in the army," said Lottie as she took a biscuit from the plate.

"That's right, he was until about five years ago and that's when he, Marlene and the children moved down here. It might be more than five years but they were here well before us anyway."

"Any idea what job he had in the army?" Hetty was thinking guns.

"I don't know nor do I know his rank. He likes cooking though but that doesn't mean that's what he did."

"So what does he do now?" Hetty asked.

"He works in a builders merchants but I don't know where."

"Hmm, nothing dodgy about that then," conceded Hetty.

"But we don't think Gary is the dodgy one, do we?" said Debbie, "and we don't know for sure that the Andrew who Marlene was talking to last night was Andrew Banks."

"Oh, it'll be him for sure," maintained Hetty, "I have a gut feeling. And remember having seen the red Fiesta down by the boating lake means we have every reason now to believe that he's the chap Marlene goes off with on Tuesday."

"And probably other nights as well," Lottie added.

"Maybe," agreed Debbie, "So what have you two discovered?"

"Well, we went to the pub last night after you rang hoping to see Tess because she's a mine of information, and as luck would have it she was there working."

"I didn't know Tess worked in the pub," said Debbie, "I thought she worked in Taffeta's Tea Shoppe."

"She does both, three days in the tea shop and a couple of nights in the pub."

"I see, so it must be at her places of work that she gets all her information."

"Yes, most of it," Lottie agreed, "which is very handy and of course she's also a close neighbour of Cynthia who works as a tour guide at Pentrillick House."

Debbie noticed a frown on Hetty's face. "Sorry, Hetty. I interrupted you, please continue."

"Right, well anyway, when we got to the pub we asked Tess what she knew about Andrew Banks and apparently, daft I know, but he works in a bank and it's also rumoured that he's involved in some illicit activity."

Debbie looked nonplussed. "What do you mean by illicit activity?"

"That's what we need to find out," said Hetty, "but it'll no doubt involve money because he seems to be fixated by it."

"I see. So that's why Hazel's children don't like him. They've heard rumours of his reputation."

Lottie nodded. "Spot on."

"But where does Marlene come into this?" Debbie asked.

Lottie shrugged her shoulders. "I suppose she's just his fancy piece."

Debbie smiled. "Or maybe she's an accomplice."

"Wow, yes," grinned Hetty, "I bet she is. I suggest we take a trip into Helston and watch Andrew Bank's house for a while because at the moment we only know he drives a red Ford Fiesta and works in a bank but have no idea what he looks like. Once we've seen him and probably even get a picture of him on our phones we can look into his activities more closely."

"When is Gideon next working, Debbie?" Lottie asked.

"Not until Monday morning."

"That's only a few days away so we'll go to Helston on Monday then."

Debbie frowned. "But even if we find out more about this Andrew chap who appears to meet up with Marlene on bingo nights, what can be the connection with him and the attack on my Gideon? Not to mention the attempted murder of Hazel."

"Well we know that Andrew is a bit of a playboy and he no doubt has several women he strings along. So the connection is that both Marlene and Hazel are/were his women and I reckon he took a shot at Hazel to shut her up because she'd sussed out some of his illegal or dodgy doings."

"Reasonable theory, but why attack Gideon?" Debbie was clearly confused.

"Perhaps there is no connection," suggested Lottie, "and Gideon's attack was because he disturbed a robbery and Hazel's attack was to shut her up."

"In which case," sighed Debbie, "at the moment we suspect Andrew Banks of attempting to murder Hazel but the person who attacked Gideon is unknown."

"Correct." Hetty saw Debbie was frowning. "What's bothering you, Debbie?"

"The car," she replied. "If Andrew Banks is bit of a playboy why does he drive a modest car like a Fiesta?"

"Hmm, good point," gasped Lottie, "that doesn't seem logical, Het."

"He must have two cars," reasoned Hetty, "remember the Fiesta was parked out on the tarmac so I expect he'll have a posh car in the garage. Probably a Porsche or whatever flashy blokes drive."

"Well whatever, we still have plenty of investigating to do," said Lottie, "although I expect the police will have checked out Andrew Banks and cleared him of suspicion as regards Hazel's assault because her children are sure to have told them about their mother's liaison with him and their suspicions of him being a crook."

"Good point," agreed Hetty, "In which case he must have a false alibi for when Hazel was shot at or have hired a hitman."

"Hitmen are usually good shots, aren't they?" giggled Debbie.

Lottie suddenly burst into peals of laughter. "That's a good point, Debbie," She looked at her sister, "Oh, Het, whatever would our parents say if they could hear us talking about hitmen and murder?"

Hetty smiled. "Remembering Mum's inquisitive nature - she'd be right behind us. She had a suspicious mind and was often right with her theories regarding the antics of our neighbours."

"Ah," said Debbie, "I see where you get it from then."

Chapter Twenty

On Saturday the nineteenth of May, despite the fact it was a glorious sunny day, many of the ladies in the village chose to be indoors watching their television sets for the wedding of Meghan Markle and Prince Harry. Hetty and Lottie watched it with Kitty and Debbie while Kitty's husband, Tommy cut the grass and cleaned the windows at their home in Blackberry Way. Gideon was working at Pentrillick House.

In the afternoon, Hetty took Albert for a walk through the village, past the Pentrillick Hotel and out into the open countryside. When they reached the signpost pointing to a hamlet named Little Trenwyn they turned round and made their way back. As they passed Sea View Cottage, Alina pulled up in Brett's car.

"Beautiful day," said the actress as she took two bags of shopping from the boot of the car, "they were very lucky for the wedding."

"Yes, they were. Very lucky indeed. Windsor looked beautiful this morning which is a great advert for this country."

Alina laughed. "Yes, but we'll not tell anyone that it's often wet and windy here."

"And not to mention cold," Hetty shuddered, "I hope we don't have another winter like the last one for a while."

"Well, if we do I'll get Brett to whisk me away in search of the sun." She closed the boot.

"Alright for some," chuckled Hetty as she continued along the pavement.

As Hetty neared the post office she stopped and looked in the window where a notice informed people that tickets for *Murder at Mulberry Hall* were available inside the shop. She felt a pang of pride and with a huge smile on her face continued along the road with a spring in her step. As she passed the fish and chip shop she sniffed the air but the temptation to go inside was overcome when she heard the wailing of sirens in the distance. The smile on her face faded and a frown took its place; the spring in her step came to an abrupt halt. She paused and listened. The noise was very close and then it stopped. Hetty resumed her walk at a much quicker pace and as she went round a bend in the main street she saw two police cars were pulled up on the road outside the charity shop along with an ambulance. Her quickened pace became a trot. On the pavement Daisy sat on a ledge beneath the shop window. Her face was white and she was being comforted by two paramedics while the door of the shop was being forced open by two police officers.

"Daisy, what's wrong?" Hetty felt her eyes watering.

"I only popped out for a while to get some milk so we could have a cup of tea. I suppose I was gone for about fifteen minutes. It would've been less but I saw Tess and so we had a bit of a natter." Daisy jumped at the sound of breaking glass, "When I got back the shop door was locked and the 'closed' sign was up. It made no sense so I rang Maisie to see where she was and ask why she'd locked up. She didn't answer so I looked in through the door and could just make out her feet sticking out from under the coat rack." Daisy burst into tears.

"What! Oh, my goodness, I hope she's alright?" As the police officers opened the door and ran inside, Hetty sat down on the pavement before her legs gave way. The paramedics went in after the police and a policewoman took their place beside Daisy.

Hetty took Daisy's hand and looked at the woman police officer. "Can you please go and find out if she's alive?"

The police officer nodded. "Okay, you two wait here."

When she came out she forced a smile but her eyes looked sombre. "Yes, she is alive but unconscious and I can't say more than that."

"We understand," whispered Hetty, "thank you."

Daisy dried her eyes.

"So what on earth can have happened?" Hetty wondered.

"Well she can't have had an accident because if she had the shop door wouldn't have been locked, would it?"

"Oh my God, I hadn't thought of that. It looks like she's been attacked then." Hetty felt sick.

"Yes, it does," sniffed Daisy, "but who could have done such a thing?"

Hetty stayed with Daisy until her husband arrived; she then walked home. She was still shaking when she arrived back at Primrose Cottage and told her sister what had happened.

"I'm really confused now, Lottie, really I am. What on earth is going on?"

"I wish I knew. It makes no sense. Shall I ring Debbie and tell her?"

"Not for a while. I want to sit quietly and think. You know, see if I can fathom it out."

On Sunday after church the sisters learned from Kitty that Maisie was making good progress and was due to be discharged from hospital on Monday morning.

"Thank God," sighed Hetty.

"So what exactly happened?" Lottie asked.

Kitty shrugged her shoulders. "Goodness knows. Daisy said she had been tied up with scarves and had a pillowcase over her head."

"What!" Hetty gasped.

"But that's dreadful," said Lottie.

"I know. It's thought she was getting things ready for their afternoon tea because the box of broken biscuits given to them by Vicar Sam's mother, lay on the floor beside her along with a box of teabags."

"So someone must have crept up behind her," reasoned Lottie.

"Looks that way, yes."

"Was anything taken?" Hetty asked.

"Not from the till," replied Kitty.

"But something must have been taken from the shop or why would anyone have gone to such lengths?"

"I don't know," conceded Kitty, "and Daisy is still too shaken to have a thorough look. Tommy went down to see if he could see anything obvious that was missing, but only working the odd day there he's not as familiar with the stock as Daisy and Maisie. Personally I think theft is highly unlikely. I mean security in the shop is pretty lax so unless an item targeted is very large it wouldn't be difficult to slip it into a bag."

"Yes, you're quite right there," Hetty agreed.

"So had any dodgy looking people been in the shop that day?" Lottie asked. "You know, someone acting in a furtive manner or something like that?"

"Well, no. In fact what with the Royal wedding and the lovely weather, Daisy said they'd had a very quiet day and the last customer to have been in was Lucy Lacey and that was just after lunch."

"Lucy," repeated Lottie, "I wonder what she wanted."

Kitty laughed. "Nothing sinister. Apparently she wanted a new dress because she's going somewhere special. Daisy said she tried one on that took her fancy and it looked lovely so she bought it and left the shop in very high spirits."

Early on Monday morning, as pre-arranged, Hetty and Lottie picked up Debbie from St Mary's Avenue after Gideon had gone to work and the three of them then drove into Helston. They parked in the car park and then sauntered along the road, all with fingers crossed that they would see Andrew Banks. As they approached his house Lottie pointed to his red Fiesta parked in the driveway. Automatically they slowed their pace and when they reached his gate, Hetty removed her left shoe on pretence of having a stone in it. To their amazement right on cue, a man emerged from the house whistling tunelessly and walked towards the car. Lottie quickly took out her phone and pretended to take a picture of Debbie who pouted and posed to make it seem realistic.

"Got him," she whispered, as Hetty replaced her shoe. "Let's move on quick."

They walked swiftly along the road conscious that Andrew Banks was about to pull out from his driveway. To their delight they had the added bonus of him driving past them.

"I can't believe we were that lucky," laughed Hetty, as the car disappeared from view, "It was all so simple."

"Show us the picture?" gabbled Debbie, excitedly, "I want to see what he looks like as I only got a glimpse."

They all huddled around Lottie's phone.

"He doesn't look like a ladies' man," sighed Lottie, clearly disappointed, "In fact he looks very ordinary."

"Well, I suppose he's off to work at the bank or something like that," opined Hetty, "so he wouldn't want to look like a playboy, would he?"

"No, I suppose not."

Hetty put on her reading glasses to take a closer look. "How old do you reckon he is?"

"I'd say in his forties," said Debbie. Lottie agreed.

"So that makes him younger than Hazel," calculated Hetty, "because she's fifty three."

"Hence the playboy label," reasoned Lottie.

"I would have thought toy boy would have been more apt," suggested Hetty.

Debbie shook her head. "No, anything goes now and quite rightly too. Age should never be a factor in a relationship."

"Yes, I suppose you're right," Lottie returned the phone to her handbag. "Come on, let's go home and discuss it further with a nice cup of tea."

In the evening, Hetty and Lottie went to the play rehearsal. They arrived early because they were determined not to miss anything Marlene might say or do. But to their dismay she seemed concerned only with playing her part and not once mentioned anything other than the performance which was just a week away.

On Tuesday evening Hetty, Lottie and Debbie all went to bingo and although they saw Marlene picked up outside the post office as usual, they were unable to learn any more than they already knew.

"How can we further our investigations?" Lottie asked, as they sat in the Crown and Anchor after bingo.

"Perhaps we ought to forget trying to pin Hazel's attempted murder on Andrew Banks for a while and focus on the attacks on Gideon and Maisie instead," suggested Hetty.

Debbie nodded. "I'd certainly like to know who was responsible for hurting my Gideon. The police haven't any idea because there are no clues."

"But they know the mysterious fragrance was musk now," Lottie reminded her.

"Yes, but unfortunately it's not a great deal of help."

"No, I suppose not but at least there's a motive for your Gideon's attack," stated Hetty, "unlike the peculiar incident at the charity shop. I can't for the life of me see what that was all about. I mean, no money was taken from the shop till so robbery wasn't the reason nor had Maisie got into an argument with a customer or anything like that and according to Daisy the shop was very quiet on Saturday because of the Royal wedding and the lovely weather and no-one was in there when she popped out to the village store for milk anyway."

Debbie sighed. "Very odd. Goodness knows what the police must make of it."

Hetty glanced across the bar to where Paul from Saltwater House sat talking to her next door neighbour, Alex. "It's just a thought," she whispered, "but I wonder if Paul is involved at all. I mean, no-one seems to know much about him and his name is on our list albeit a late addition and what's more we know he likes sweetly scented musk because his bathroom reeks of it."

"Funny you should say that," Debbie lowered her voice, "because it had crossed my mind that it might have been him that swapped my Gideon's tonic and gin for gin and tonic seeing as how he spent a lot of his time tinkering with the bottles and so forth."

"But why would he have done that?" Lottie asked.

"I can only assume to try and stop Gideon telling the police he'd recognised the mystery scent," said Debbie.

Hetty gasped. "Which means he would be the one who your Gideon disturbed in the church."

"So are you implying that Paul was trying to pinch the silver chalice?" laughed Lottie, "because if you are that's silly. I mean, look at him. I get the impression he's quite prosperous enough without needing to nick a bit of silver to turn it into cash."

Debbie laughed. "Yes, that is silly because in retrospect he wasn't even in Cornwall when Gideon was attacked."

"He wasn't in Pentrillick but he might have been staying elsewhere in the county," persisted Hetty, "I recall saying that once before."

Debbie sighed. "I think we need to forget this line of thought and return to Hazel and Andrew Banks because at least we know Andrew's dodgy."

"Allegedly," Lottie added.

"Yes, allegedly," agreed Debbie.

Hetty frowned. "There is someone else we've forgotten and that's Brett. Remember Lottie, we saw him with a pretty brunette standing in the Mall watching the end of the London Marathon so there might be more to him than meets the eye."

Lottie laughed. "Two timing Alina doesn't make him a would-be robber or an assassin, Het."

"I agree," said Debbie, "so let's get back to Andrew because we've more to go on with him. Having said that I suppose because he's not been charged with the attempted murder of Hazel the police must already have ruled him out even if we haven't."

"Well, they might not have ruled him out completely. They might be just biding their time until they can nail him," Lottie suggested.

"So what do we do now?" Debbie asked.

"Goodness knows," admitted Hetty, "but we can't give up having got this close."

Lottie choked on her wine. "What do you mean by this close, Het? We're no nearer knowing who any of the bad blokes are today than we were when the offences took place."

"My money's still on Andrew Banks," stated Hetty, ignoring her sister, "We just need to catch him out. Catch him red-handed."

"Red-handed," chuckled Lottie, "Doing what?"

Hetty scowled as she tried to think of a logical reply.

Debbie licked her finger and then slowly ran it around the rim of her wine glass and caused it to squeak. "It's just a thought but next Tuesday instead of going to bingo why don't we follow Andrew and Marlene and see where they go? We could wait in the pub car park for them to drive by and then follow."

Hetty's jaw gaped open. "Of course. Why didn't we think of that before? That's a brilliant idea."

"We'd have to use your car though," insisted Debbie, "because Marlene would recognise mine."

"No problem," confirmed Hetty.

Lottie scowled. "But what will it achieve?"

"They might go to a pub or something like that," declared Debbie, "in which case we can follow them in, sit nearby and eavesdrop."

"We'll need to be in disguise," blurted Hetty, excitedly, "Andrew Banks wouldn't recognise us but Marlene would."

"You two are bonkers," laughed Lottie, as she drained her glass, "Anyway, there isn't any bingo next week it's been cancelled. Remember, Tuesday night will be the final practice for the play in the village hall before the dress rehearsal on Wednesday so Marlene will definitely be at that and not gadding off out with Andrew Banks. After all she is the leading lady."

"Damn," spluttered Hetty, "Oh well, we'll leave it until the week after then."

Chapter Twenty One

The weather forecast for the late May Bank Holiday and half term week was warm, dry and sunny and the good weather looked set to continue well into June. Inside Primrose Cottage on Saturday morning, Lottie was busy in the kitchen making cakes for the arrival of her grandchildren the following day and outside Hetty was in the greenhouse staking the tomato and chilli plants. As she worked she thought, her thoughts dominated by the unsolved crimes in the village. After their chores were finished the sisters went out into the back garden and sat by the pond with mugs of coffee.

"I know it's daft," confessed Hetty, as she sat fanning herself with the latest batch of junk mail she had just picked up off the doormat, "but the only connection for all the crimes I can come up with is broken biscuits."

"What! That's ridiculous. I suppose you're basing your claim on the silly things Lucy Lacey said."

"They weren't silly. Many of them came true but I'm thinking more along the lines of broken biscuits being present in one way or another with all of the incidents."

"You can't be serious. Besides broken biscuits weren't present in all cases. In fact only Gideon had them as I recall."

Hetty shook her head. "No, you're wrong, Lottie. I've just been thinking it through. In the case of Hazel she'd just made biscuits and knocked them onto the floor as she fled from the kitchen which would have caused them to break. As regards Gideon getting drunk, I reckon that was deliberate and done by someone, possibly Paul, who wanted to take Gideon's mind off recognising the smell of musk. Remember Nicki said his drink was really strong so without doubt someone must have topped up his glass when he wasn't looking and so that he was drinking near neat gin without realising it."

"Hang on a minute. We talked about this the other day but I'm baffled as to where broken biscuits come into it."

"Vicar Sam brought a box of biscuits with him and gave them to Maisie and Daisy to enjoy in the charity shop. Surely you remember that? He said he'd been meaning to drop it into the shop for some time but kept forgetting. It was the last box."

Lottie struggled to keep a straight face. "Yes, I remember and I suppose you want to blame those biscuits for Maisie's assault as well?"

"Well yes, because Maisie went to the shop to buy milk for their tea to have with the broken biscuits and Daisy said the box of biscuits was on the floor when they found Maisie."

"Along with a box of teabags."

"That's right. I'm glad you pay attention to these minor details because they're often the clues that get overlooked."

"I think you've been in the sun too long, Het. You're losing your ability to think straight."

"Well, can you come up with anything better?"

"No."

"Oh Lottie, I'm just trying to make sense of all this."

"I know you are, Het, and it's a good effort but it's daft, bonkers, crackers, and even if there is a shred of truth in it, it doesn't in any way point us towards the person or persons responsible for committing any of these crimes, does it?"

"No." Hetty looked downcast.

"Cheer up. It'll no doubt get solved one day and then we'll say we can't believe that we never thought of whoever it is."

When leaving the church on Sunday morning, Lottie noticed that the hem of Vicar Sam's surplice was held up with a safety pin.

"Oh, Sam, would you like me to mend that for you?" she asked, "It won't take many minutes."

The vicar looked at the hem. "Oh dear, does it show? I pinned it up as a temporary measure thinking Mum could mend it when she gets here later this week. I can do most chores around the house, you see, but sewing isn't one of them. It's too fiddly."

"Well, I love sewing so I'm more than happy to do it."

"That might be best then because with the play and decorating the church both taking place this week I might well forget to ask Mum anyway."

"Of course. So shall I call round at the Vicarage to pick it up?"

"No, because I won't be taking it home with me it'll be here in the church."

"On the pegs with the choir's cassocks and so forth?"

"No, there's a cupboard in the vestry that I use as a wardrobe. It'll be in that."

"Oh, that's easy then," said Lottie, "and I can pick it up tomorrow when Hetty and I come down to the church to unlock to let the chap with the scaffold tower in."

"Excellent idea. I'd forgotten you were doing that. You know where the church keys are kept I assume."

Lottie laughed. "Yes, you have one and the spare is hidden inside the large urn on the grave of Henry Lobb who died in 1707 and is buried near to the old yew tree."

"And there's a slate on top of the urn to keep the rain out," Hetty added.

"That's right. We chose Henry to be our key keeper because there is no fear of a family member turning up to put flowers on his grave now. I understand the Lobbs left the village two hundred years ago."

In the afternoon, Hetty and Lottie drove to Penzance to meet Zac and the twins at the railway station. The train was on time and the children were all in high spirits.

"Good journey?" asked Lottie as they walked along the platform.

"Yes, although it wasn't straightforward like last summer because apparently they do electrification work at the weekends ready for the new trains so the journey took longer than usual but we knew it was going to anyway. I was reading all about it online, you see. You're going to have new super-duper Hitachi trains soon and they'll be green. I've seen pictures and they look terrific." Zac looked for a picture on his phone.

"Really, but I like the old purple ones," said Hetty, looking back along the length of the train, "I like their style too although it's been around for a while. Must be forty years or more."

"Do trains come in styles?" Lottie teased, as they reached the end of the platform.

"Don't be awkward, Lottie. You know what I mean."

"Purple?" Zac queried, looking up from his phone, "The train looks blue to me."

"And me," Lottie agreed.

"No, it's definitely purple," insisted Hetty.

"I hope you've all remembered the books you'll need for revision," gushed Lottie, eager to change the subject.

Kate laughed. "As if Mum would let us forget. She must have checked we had them a hundred times."

"And then Dad checked too," Vicki added.

"Good, so you're ready to put in lots of hard work."

"We don't have much choice," sighed Kate, "Mum and Dad have both agreed that if we don't do well in our exams it'll be because we've idled away this week."

"So you have to get good grades to prove you can be trusted," laughed Hetty, "There are no flies on your parents."

In the village hall on Sunday afternoon, Ian the electrician with the help of Sid finished putting up lights for the production of *Murder at Mulberry Hall*.

"You've got a busy week ahead what with painting the church and working the lights," commented Sid, as he moved around on different parts of the stage to make sure the lights shone in the right places.

"I'm actually looking forward to it. It'll make a nice change. You're going to be pretty busy yourself if you're on stage each night after a day's work."

"No, I won't be doing that because I've taken the week off," said Sid, "that's the beauty of being self-employed. Mind you I won't get paid for it as you well know."

"Yes, that's the downside. Still, I wouldn't have it any other way. I like to be me own boss."

"Same here."

"That's great, Sid, thanks." Ian switched off the light's control panel. "So what's it like playing the part of a detective inspector?"

"I rather like it," confessed Sid, as he jumped down from the stage, "Makes me feel a bit important, if you see what I mean and I've got some great lines."

"So do you actually solve the crime or are you an incompetent nincompoop?"

Sid laughed. "Bit of both. I'm not the brightest pebble on the beach but I get there in the end."

"Sounds like they could do with your character to sort out the goings on round here then. I can't believe no-one's been arrested for any of the crimes, or even taken in for questioning as far as I know."

"Well, I think the coppers play it all pretty close to their chests and since no-one's been killed they haven't got the media putting pressure on them by saying there's a murderer at large."

"Hmm, that's as maybe but I don't think the person who took a pot shot at Hazel Mitchell intended her to live."

"No I suppose not but she did survive so it hasn't made the headlines."

"What about the incident in the charity shop? Have you heard any more about that?"

Sid, feeling warm, rolled up his shirt sleeves. "I don't know any more than what's doing the rounds but I did have a brief chat with Maisie at the last rehearsal and it looks like she's made a full recovery because she said she feels ninety nine percent fit now."

"Pleased to hear that," said Ian, "So is she in the play then?"

"No, she's doing costumes with Lottie Burton."

"I see, so can she remember anything useful about the bizarre attack on her?"

Sid shook his head. "Sadly not, so there's even less to go on than there is with Gideon."

"And Hazel too."

"I've heard Tristan's going to get CCTV all over the grounds of Pentrillick House now and in every room too, whether they're used or not," stated Sid.

"Sadly though it's closing the door after the horse has bolted."

Sid grinned. "Yes, but there's always the possibility of another crime so Tristan's not taking any risks."

Ian looked at his watch. "I've heard rumours that they suspect an old boyfriend of Hazel's being involved somehow or other."

Sid was astounded. "Old boyfriend. How old? She's only been widowed a couple of years. Surely they're not looking back to before she was married."

"No, no, it's someone she's been knocking around with since she lost her husband. Probably nothing in it though. You know how folks make things up if they don't know what's going on."

"Hmm, fake news. Seems to be rife at the moment in all walks of life."

Ian picked up his tool box. "Fancy a pint?"

"Sounds like a good idea."

"Come on then, we're done here. I'll pop this back in the van then we'll walk down to the pub."

Chapter Twenty Two

On Bank Holiday Monday morning, Zac and the twins sat in the sitting room of Primrose Cottage quietly revising. They didn't object for the weather was glorious and they were all eager to get the studies over and done with so they could go outside. While they studied, their grandmother and great aunt made a picnic lunch for them to take to the beach.

In the afternoon, Hetty and Lottie walked down to the church and retrieved the key from its custodian, Henry Lobb, and shortly after they had unlocked the church the scaffold tower was delivered by Ian the electrician's friend. The plan was that Ian and Sid would then erect the tower in the evening ready for Ian to start painting on Wednesday morning.

While the equipment was laid out on the church aisle, Lottie who had a needle, white cotton and scissors in her handbag, sat on the old wooden chest in the vestry and mended the vicar's surplice rather than take it home. It didn't take long for the scaffold to be dropped off and by the time it was done, Lottie had finished her mending.

After Hetty had said goodbye to and thanked Ian's friend she returned to the vestry where Lottie was slipping Vicar Sam's surplice onto a coat hanger. As she closed the cupboard door they heard the church door open and footsteps as someone walked up the main aisle of the church. Quietly, Lottie returned the needle, scissors and cotton to her handbag. Hetty raised her fingers to her lips. "Shush, let's nip out there," she whispered, "then if it's someone up to no good we can catch them red-handed."

Lottie nodded and placed her handbag on top of the old chest. Both women then dashed out determined to apprehend whoever it was. To their annoyance the person in question fled down the aisle and out of the door but not before they'd had a chance to glimpse a tall, slim figure with long blonde hair.

"Alina," gasped Hetty, as the church door slammed shut, "that was Alina."

"Yes, it was but whatever was she doing in here?"

Hetty folded her arms. "Up to no good do you think?"

"Well, I can't see why and I daresay if we asked her she'd have a perfectly good reason."

"Yes, but if that's the case why did she run away?"

"I've no idea but if she's at tonight's practice we must ask her."

"There isn't a practice tonight, Lottie. Remember Robert said we could all have the night off since it's Bank Holiday."

"Okay, we'll ask her tomorrow then."

"I'm not waiting that long," hissed Hetty, taking her mobile phone from the pocket of her tunic, "I'm going to report it to the police right now. It's the proper thing to do because I know they're desperate for any information and keep telling us to report anything which might help with their enquiries no matter how small."

"I don't think you should, Het."

"Well, I disagree." She selected the number of the local police stored on her phone.

"On your head be it," tutted Lottie, as she went back into the vestry to collect her handbag, "but I think you might live to regret it."

When Brett returned from a visit to the Crown and Anchor where he'd had a drink with Paul, he was surprised to see a police car parked outside Sea View Cottage. Inside he found

Alina in the hallway bidding two police officers farewell. His eyebrows rose. "Is everything okay?"

Alina giggled. "Yes, everything's fine, Brett. Just a little misunderstanding that's all." She turned to the officers. "I'll explain to my boyfriend. Thank you for calling."

"Our pleasure," they said in unison, "and thank you for your co-operation and thank you for the tea."

Brett watched as Alina closed the front door. "What was that all about? I thought you wanted a quiet afternoon to finish reading the book you've been engrossed in these past few days."

"Come and sit down and I'll tell you."

They sat in armchairs on either side of the hearth. "This afternoon after you'd gone off to the pub and after I'd finished reading the book, I walked over to the church. I wanted to go inside, you see, because the other day you told me how beautiful the interior is and the stained glass windows in particular. I knew it was unlocked because from the upstairs window I had seen a man with a van parked outside going back and forth with something or other."

"Probably Ian's mate, the one who's loaning the tower so that Ian can decorate the church."

"Ah, yes, I expect it was. Anyway, I thought I'd nip over before someone came to lock up." She giggled, "I didn't really get a chance to see much though because as I was walking up the aisle I sensed that I wasn't alone. It was really spooky. The hairs on the back of my neck stood up, I slowed down and then stopped abruptly because two shadows suddenly flew out from the vestry. I was absolutely terrified. I panicked and ran away as quickly as possible and didn't stop 'til I got back here. I thought it was the person who had attacked the organist you see but didn't want to hang around to find out if it was or wasn't."

"Okay, that makes sense but why were the police here?"

Alina blushed. "Because it turns out that the two shadows who frightened me were thinking along the same lines. They thought I might be the person who attacked the organist and took the candlesticks and because I ran away that convinced them that I was up to no good. I feel so silly and no doubt they will too."

"Oh dear," tutted Brett. "What a to-do. Any idea who the two shadows were?"

Alina smiled sweetly. "Oh yes, according to the police officers they were your Mrs Appleby and her sister."

Brett laughed. "You don't surprise me there."

After their visit to Sea View Cottage, the two police officers drove up to Primrose Cottage to inform the sisters the reason why Alina was in the church and more importantly, why she fled.

"Oh dear," mumbled Hetty as the police car drove away, "I do hope Brett doesn't get to hear of this. I don't think he'll be very impressed to learn we tried to implicate his girlfriend in assault."

"And robbery."

"Oh don't."

"And attempted murder, I suppose," said Lottie, trying to supress the desire to laugh, "I mean, I know you, Debbie and me all agree that the person who attacked Gideon was not the person who shot Hazel because we think that was Andrew Banks but it's quite possible that we're wrong and the same person might have committed both crimes and even attacked poor Maisie too."

Hetty groaned.

"I told you not to report it, Het but you wouldn't listen, but then you always were impetuous."

"Do you think I'll get the sack?"

"What at this short notice? It's the dress rehearsal on Wednesday so it's far too late to replace you." Lottie softened, "Besides you're a damn good Mrs Appleby and there's no-one in the village to better you. Having said that, I think you ought to give Brett a wide berth for a while and hope he forgets."

"But he doesn't have long to forget, does he? Tomorrow is the last practice before the dress rehearsal so I'm bound to see him then."

Later in the afternoon the telephone rang in the hallway of Primrose Cottage. Lottie, who was walking through to the kitchen, answered it. It was Debbie.

"Oh, Lottie," she squealed, "Gideon's just come back from Pentrillick House and he's really, really excited because of the latest news doing the rounds down there. I won't tell you what it is but suggest you watch the local news which is on shortly because it's bound to be included. I promise you'll be fascinated. I'm in shock. I can't believe it."

"Whatever can she be talking about?" wondered Hetty, after Lottie had relayed the news.

"Perhaps they've found out who's been committing all the crimes round here at last," suggested Vicki, "It's about time someone was arrested for them."

"Maybe," conceded Hetty, "but we don't think they were all committed by the same person. Having said that, perhaps they were."

"Well at least we know it's not Alina," chuckled Lottie.

Hetty squirmed.

Kate frowned. "How do you know it's not her? I mean, I don't expect it is but it could be."

Lottie explained what had happened earlier in the day while her grandchildren were out.

"That's brilliant. I must remember to tell Dad when we get home," giggled Vicki, "he'll think it's hilarious."

"Oh, please don't," begged Hetty, "because he'll never let me live it down."

"Well. It might slip my mind if I don't have to wash up tonight."

"Victoria Burton you get more like me every day," spluttered Hetty.

Zac glanced at the clock on the mantelpiece. "Only ten minutes to go 'til the local news is on and then we'll find out what your friend Debbie was on about."

The family all sat quietly as the news began and to their surprise, the arrest of a Helston man was mentioned in the headlines. When the story began it stated the arrested man was fifty one year old Andrew Banks who was a member of a sought after gang who allegedly made and distributed counterfeit bank notes. Mr Banks worked in a local bank where he had been under surveillance for some time. The programme didn't give any more details other than to show a picture of the arrested man.

"That's not Andrew Banks," screamed Hetty, sitting forward in her chair, "you took a picture of him didn't you, Lottie?"

"I took a picture of someone who we thought was Andrew Banks," said Lottie, trying to make sense of the news, "But it's quite obvious we were wrong."

"But the man we pictured is the man who Marlene goes out with because we recognised his car."

"That's as maybe but he clearly isn't Andrew Banks." Lottie took out her phone to check the picture she had taken and then showed it to her sister. The children gathered around too. "They're nothing like each other, Het," hissed Lottie.

The twins giggled.

Hetty's cheeks glowed crimson. "Oh, no, poor man. Thank goodness we didn't accost him or anything like that."

"Heaven forbid. I wonder who he is though. This chap on my phone, that is."

"Well, I suppose he's just Marlene's fancy man or something like that."

"Yes, anyway, whatever, there's no way he's involved in any of the goings on in this village so I shall delete his picture."

Hetty stood up. "And I'm going to ring Debbie to see if she knows any more details."

"Good idea. It's frustrating only knowing half the story."

"Well, well, well," tutted Hetty as she put down the phone and returned to the sitting room, "what a rogue." She sat down. "Apparently he's not a local man at all but he's been in the area for a couple of years. The gang of crooks he works with are up-country somewhere or other, Debbie doesn't know where. Apparently after the notes are printed they're taken by various members to different parts of the country and dispersed in dribs and drabs. Andrew Banks got roped in because he worked for a bank where it was his job to keep the cash machine topped up. So what he did was put fake notes in the machine every day having already swapped them beforehand with untraceable used notes."

"Wow," uttered Vicki.

Lottie looked shocked. "Well, I suppose Hazel's children will be delighted that their suspicions were justified but Hazel herself will be mortified if and when she regains consciousness."

"Ah yes, and that's another thing," said Hetty, "she has. The doctors brought her out of the medically induced coma this morning and she seems to be making good progress."

"Thank goodness for that," sighed Lottie, much relieved, "Positive news at last. Perhaps we might get somewhere now."

Detective Inspector Fox sat down at his desk and leaned back in his chair with his hands firmly clasped behind his head. At last Andrew Banks was under lock and key, now he just needed to wind up the Pentrillick crimes although he knew that was likely to be less straight forward. The assault on Gideon Elms was he believed the result of a disturbed robbery so he thought it best to leave that incident for a while and concentrate instead on the attempted murder of Hazel Mitchell.

He looked over the case notes. Staff at Pentrillick House had been questioned and shown pictures of Andrew Banks but no-one recalled seeing him hanging around the property in the days before the attempted murder. However, one member of staff, a Cynthia Watkins who works as a tour guide confirmed that Mrs Mitchell and Andrew Banks were friends and met frequently. When asked if Mrs Mitchell ever expressed any concerns about Banks she said only that she was afraid her two children might find out about the meetings and that they disapproved of him.

Detective Inspector Fox sighed. As much as he would like to be able to pin the attempted murder of Hazel Mitchell on Andrew Banks he knew there was no evidence to back it up. Furthermore, Banks had a sound alibi for the afternoon Mrs Mitchell was shot. He was up-country collecting counterfeit bank notes and the force had the surveillance footage to prove it. Although of course, Andrew Banks had given them a different alibi and claimed he was visiting a mate on Easter Monday afternoon and when questioned, the dodgy mate had vouched for him. Of course it was possible that Andrew Banks had hired a hitman to dispose of Mrs Mitchell but all evidence pointed to it being the act of someone who was not used to handling a gun.

Then there was the strange affair at the charity shop. That made no sense at all. In fact, all three cases in Pentrillick were peculiar. Was there a link between them or were they looking for three individuals?

A knock on his office door caused Detective Inspector Fox to lean forward. "Come in," he bellowed.

WPC Jenkins entered the office. "Sir, we've got results back from the lab and fibres found on the scarves in the charity shop matches those found on the church curtain. So it looks as though the same person committed both crimes."

"Hmm, interesting. So we have two attempted robberies committed by the same person during which he took nothing other than a pair of brass candlesticks which were later found discarded on the beach in Pentrillick."

"Looks that way, sir."

"But why?"

"Don't know, sir. Wish I did. Although I suppose it might have been kids who did it for a lark or even a dare."

"Even that's a possibility but knowing kids I'm sure they'd have been tempted to steal something. Perhaps not from the church but definitely from the charity shop where there was money in the till."

"Very true, sir."

"Yet the till was not touched."

"No, sir."

"So can you tell me what the lab think the fibres are from?"

"A finely knitted black woollen garment, sir."

"Hmm, so not very helpful at this stage. Okay, thank you, Jenkins. At least we know now that we're only looking for two people and that one of them owns a black finely knitted garment."

"Two," repeated WPC Jenkins, "but we agree the same person did both."

"Yes, the same person is responsible for the two pointless robberies but there is another person out there who attempted to murder Hazel Mitchell the cook at Pentrillick House."

"Of course, I'm not on the Mitchell case, sir, so it slipped my memory."

Chapter Twenty Three

"We're going down to the church at eleven o'clock to help the vicar and other volunteers undress the altar and move things ready for the decorating," said Lottie, on Wednesday morning as the family sat round the table eating breakfast, "Do you girls have plans for the day?"

The twins looked at each other, their eyes like saucers. "We were going to go for a swim after we've done our revision," gushed Vicki, "but perhaps we could go with you and help with the church stuff and then go swimming later."

"I wonder why," teased Zac.

Vicki sitting opposite her brother, aimed a kicked at his shin beneath the table.

"That's very sweet of you," said Lottie, missing the reason for the girls' enthusiasm, "I'm sure your efforts will be greatly appreciated."

"We like to help," declared Kate, "and Mum and Dad both said to make ourselves useful while we're here."

"How about you, Zac. Do you have plans for today?" Hetty asked.

"Yes, Emma and me are going down Penzance way, wind surfing."

Hetty tutted. "Well, you tell Emma to be careful. We don't want any of the cast with broken bones this week and it's the dress rehearsal tonight."

Zac laughed. "She's been before and is actually quite good but I'll tell her what you said."

Ian had already started to paint the main body of the church when they arrived and while he worked they helped the other volunteers undress the altar, roll up the carpets in the chancel and sanctuary and take removable objects into the vestry.

"Thank you for mending my surplice," said Vicar Sam to Lottie, as he lifted a heavy bible from the lectern. "You've done a splendid job. So neat I can't even tell which bit had come undone."

"My pleasure."

"Are your parents here yet?" Hetty asked.

"No not until Friday, so you've a couple more days yet to finish off the broken biscuits."

Hetty laughed. "They've been very welcome. In fact I don't think any of them were disliked."

"The chocolate ones are the best," said Kate: "they're really yummy."

As Sam and Tommy carried out a rolled up carpet, Vicki looked at the vast expanse of stone floor. "It looks very bare now and it echoes too. Quite spooky."

"That's because the carpets muffle the sound," remarked Kitty, "and I agree with you, it does feel spooky."

"It feels and looks cold too," chuntered Hetty, rubbing her arms, "in fact I wish I'd put a cardigan on."

"Well, we've finished now," said the vicar, "so you can all go out and enjoy the beautiful sunshine but don't overdo it, Hetty, we've got a big night tonight."

"Yes, the dress rehearsal. I can't wait."

"Ought we not to put dust sheets over the altar before we go?" Kitty asked, "Because we don't want it splashed with paint."

"Definitely," Sam agreed. "I'm glad you thought of that. There are some in the belfry I'll go and get them." He turned to walk down the aisle.

"Surely it'd be much simpler to pull it out and then move it around so it'd always be away from the paint pot," suggested Kate, "It'd make it easier to paint round the back of it too."

Vicar Sam stopped in his tracks. "What an excellent idea." He was clearly impressed.

Kate beamed.

Vicki scowled.

"What do you mean by pull it out?" Hetty was nonplussed, "Surely it's fixed in place."

Kate shook her head. "No I'm sure it'll come out, Auntie Het. You see, I remember when we had our church decorated back home that some of us helped by doing what we've been doing here today and we took the altar out so that the man doing the decorating could paint behind it. I was absolutely gobsmacked at the time because underneath the fancy wooden thing was the original stone altar which was much lower than the wooden one. It was awesome."

Hetty's jaw dropped.

"Ah, another good point." Sam patted Kate's shoulder, "Well done, young lady and you're quite right of course. You see, back in medieval times, church altars were rectangular slabs made of stone or in some cases even marble but after the Reformation they were replaced by wooden creations, so I suppose in the church you speak of, Kate, they simply put the new one over the top of the old."

"Really!" Kitty looked at the bare wooden altar, "So do you think the old original one might be under this one too?"

"Well, there's only one way to find out, Kitty, and I'm sure we're all equally curious now. I know I am. The idea of finding a hidden fourteenth century altar really appeals." Vicar Sam rolled up his shirt sleeves. "Give us a hand please, Tom, and we'll have a look."

Tommy took one end of the wooden altar and Sam took the other and together they lifted it down the sanctuary steps. As hoped a centuries old small stone altar was revealed. All gazed open-mouthed, but it wasn't so much the old altar that caused the wonder as the three plastic supermarket carrier bags that lay on top of it.

"Now, history might not be my best subject," said Tommy, scratching his chin, "but I'm pretty certain those carrier bags aren't fourteenth century."

Vicki giggled.

Vicar Sam shook his head. "How bizarre. I wonder how long they've been there."

"Well, aren't you going to have a look and see what's in them?" Hetty was beyond curious.

Sam nodded. "Yes, yes, I suppose I ought."

Cautiously, he approached the stone altar and gently lifted the first bag. When he looked inside he gasped. "Two ancient pistols. What on earth are they doing in here?" He held open the bag so that everyone could see inside.

In the next was a silver platter and in the third, various items of jewellery and two Fabergé eggs.

"The long lost Liddicott-Treen treasure," whispered Kitty, "I can't believe it's been here right under our noses all this time."

"Can't we tip it all out and look at it properly?" Tommy asked.

"Oh no," shrieked Kate, emphatically, "because the fingerprints of the thieves might be on some of the things."

"You're very switched on, young lady," said Vicar Sam, "and quite right too."

Kate beamed.

"So perhaps the Pentrillick House thieves were locals after all," reasoned Ian, who had climbed down from the tower on hearing of the find, "I've heard several people share that theory."

Lottie shook her head. "But if they were, why leave it here all these years?"

"Perhaps they died in an accident or something like that before they had a chance to retrieve it," suggested Kitty.

"No, no, I don't think the thieves were locals at all," revealed Hetty, as she drummed her fingers on the front of the choir stalls, "I think they were up-country buggers and this is what the person who attacked Gideon in the vestry was looking for?"

Chapter Twenty Four

On Wednesday evening, the drama group gathered in the village hall for the dress rehearsal and there was much excitement backstage as all were aware of the discovery in the church earlier in the day. There was also much relief. Hazel Mitchell having been brought out of the medically induced coma seemed to be making excellent progress and the doctors maintained there was every good reason to suppose that she would make a full recovery.

"Has Hazel been questioned by the police yet?" Daisy asked.

Alex shook his head. "Not yet, the doctors forbid it and say she must be left in peace for a few more days."

"It's possible she won't remember anything of that afternoon anyway," said Tess, as she painted her nails, "trauma can play havoc with the memory and we don't even know if she saw the face of her assailant anyway."

Hetty pinned up her hair prior to putting on her wig. "I think that with all that's happened in the last two days I'll forget my lines tonight. My head's all in a whirl especially after this morning's discovery."

Marlene chuckled. "This area's becoming a hotspot for news."

Tess replaced the lid on the bottle of nail varnish. "I bet the Liddicott-Treens feel much the same as well now that their valuables have been found. I know for a fact that Tristan never thought they'd see any of it again and he must be astonished by the unusual place in which it was hidden. I know I was and still am."

Daisy chortled. "I wouldn't have looked under the altar in a thousand years."

"The discovery clears the Liddicott-Treens' name as well," said Chloe, as she powdered her face, "and stamps out all the evil gossip about them having done it for the insurance. Not that I ever believed a word of it." She cast an accusing glance in Marlene's direction.

"But who on earth put it there and why haven't they recovered it?" Luke asked, "I can't see anyone abandoning a treasure trove like that."

"Perhaps the robber died," reasoned Tess, "and so he never got the chance to come back and collect it."

Hetty nodded. "Kitty suggested that and it is a possibility but I think he's still very much alive and it was him looking for the stuff when Gideon interrupted his search in the vestry."

"Well yes, but surely the person who hid it would know where to look which means he wouldn't have been searching through the chest in the first place," laughed Chloe.

"You're right," Daisy agreed, "so it makes no sense. No sense at all."

When Bernie emerged from the changing room dressed in dungarees, check shirt, gumboots and a straw hat, all heads turned.

"Oh my goodness," smiled Chloe, "you look so comical."

"If you think I look funny, wait 'til you see Sid, he's had me in stitches."

On cue Sid entered the room. He wore the mac found in the charity shop and on his head was the trilby hat. His moustache was heavily waxed and curled at either end. Over his eyes he wore a pair of dark sunglasses and in his hand he held a large magnifying glass.

"Brilliant," laughed Daisy, as Sid did a twirl, "you really do look the part. They'll be no confusion with the audience as to who you are meant to be."

"And it's obvious too that Bernie is the gardener," giggled Emma.

"I hope these will be alright," hissed Marlene, as she slipped on a pair of flat soft leather shoes, "they're not my usual style but they have rubber soles so I thought they might be quieter for when walking across the stage. I don't want to clomp around and sound like a herd of elephants." She winced when she stood up. "They're a bit tight as I've not worn them yet. I hope they won't cripple me."

"Very wise of you," said Tess, as she blew her nails to dry them, "and they look fine."

Hetty put on her wig and Karen brushed the grey curls. "It's very realistic, if I didn't know better I'd have thought it was your real hair."

Marlene gasped when she saw Vicar Sam dressed in his police sergeant's uniform. "My, don't you look handsome? I mean, you're a handsome man anyway but that outfit knocks socks off your vicar clobber. I have to confess though that I'm a sucker when it comes to uniforms. That's what attracted me to my Gary."

Kitty came backstage. "Are you nearly ready? Because Robert would like to get started."

Everyone said they were. "Okay, I'll tell Robert."

"Is Brett here?" Marlene asked Kitty as she turned to leave.

Kitty nodded. "Yes, he and Alina got here ten minutes ago so you have an audience of eight tonight."

"Eight?" Luke Burleigh queried.

"Yes, Brett, Alina, Robert, Lottie, Maisie, Zac and his two sisters," counted Kitty on her fingers, "oh, and Gideon and me as well when we're not playing the piano."

"Zac and the girls," laughed Tess, "how did they sneak in?"

"Robert said they could come along because they'd be at a loose end otherwise with Hetty, Lottie and Emma all involved with the production," said Kitty.

"I was only teasing," Tess chuckled, "as far as I'm concerned the more the merrier out there tonight as it'll help get us used to an audience."

The opening scene was the drawing room of the hairstylist's home and the first person to enter was Marlene who played the part of his wife. All was silent as she entered stage right carrying flowers supposedly brought in from the gardens. Half way across the stage she stopped. "Sorry," she whispered, her cheeks a bright shade of pink, "can I change my silly squeaky shoes and then start again?"

Vicki and Kate giggled and to her relief Marlene saw that Robert was in fits of laughter too. "Of course you may, off you go," he chuckled, "We don't want the audience to think there's a mouse on the stage."

"Thank you."

"Just a minute." Gideon rose from the piano stool and looked up at Marlene. "Would you walk across the stage again, please?"

"Why?"

"Please, I do have a reason albeit rather absurd."

"Okay." Marlene slowly walked across the stage clearly embarrassed by her squeaky shoes.

"That's it," gasped Gideon, gripping the piano to steady himself, "that's the pitch of squeaking noise I heard just before I was attacked in the church."

All eyes gazed at Marlene who stood open mouthed. "Well, it wasn't me. I bought these shoes sometime after your attack. They came from the charity shop. Honest, ask Maisie she served me."

Maisie nodded. "Yes, it's true, Gideon. They were amongst the stuff brought in by you, Brett."

All eyes turned to Brett.

Brett looked nonplussed. "Me. Were they? I thought everything I sent was books, household items, garden paraphernalia and stuff like that."

"It was apart from those shoes."

Faces of the cast who were waiting in the wings peered round the curtains as Brett stood and crossed to the stage his eyes fixed on Marlene's feet. He scowled, turned and then pointed at Alina who sat motionless, her face a deathly white. "They look like a pair you used to wear, Al. Are they yours?"

Alina stood as he moved closer. "And musk," he whispered, "you always used to wear a musky perfume but it's just occurred to me that of late you've moved on to a different fragrance."

The entire cast were now on the stage.

"I...I..." Alina turned and backed away. As she stumbled over a chair, her phone rang. A look of horror crossed her face and she squashed her bag against her chest in an attempt to muffle the sound.

"That's it," shouted Gideon, "that's the ring tone I heard in the vestry."

Everyone gasped.

"No, no, I," Alina took to her heels and disappeared through the open door. But Zac was too quick, he dashed after her and caught her by the arm before she reached the pavement.

It was nearly nine o'clock before the dress rehearsal finally got underway. After Zac had dragged Alina back into the hall, Brett rang the police himself and reported the suspicious behaviour of his girlfriend. Detective Inspector Fox who had just come on duty when they got the call, arrived promptly along with three other police officers. In the hall they found Alina seated in the middle of the room surrounded by a circle of people dressed in strange outfits. Robert explained they were in the hall for the dress rehearsal of a play and then the police officers questioned Brett and several members of the cast. Alina, who refused to say anything, was eventually taken away, tears streaming down her face and clearly in a state of shock. The only words she had spoken were to Brett. "Please forgive me," she'd said. Three little words that would ring in his ears over and over again.

Several of the women were tearful too, others were stunned into silence. Nobody quite knew what to say or what to do.

"I'm sorry," mumbled Brett, as they heard the police cars drive away, "I should have been more circumspect."

"Don't blame yourself," sympathised Robert, "None of us would have suspected Alina. Why should we? As far as I can see there's no motive and she's not known the area for long anyway."

Gideon was nonplussed. "I agree. I mean, why on earth would the likes of Alina have taken the candlesticks? They're not even fashionable."

"That's probably why she threw them away," reasoned Marlene, "Great cumbersome things, I wouldn't want them."

"But why take them if you don't want them," said Luke, "it doesn't make any sense."

"It certainly doesn't," Kitty sat down on the piano stools to ease her shaking limbs.

Hetty whispered to Lottie, "I can't get my head round this and even if Alina was the person who attacked Gideon she can't be responsible for the attempted murder of Hazel."

"Or the attack on poor Maisie," added Lottie.

"I think under the circumstances it would be best if we called the dress rehearsal off," sighed Robert, "I'm sure none of you are feeling up to performing."

Some were clearly disappointed.

Brett shook his head emphatically. "No, no, Robert, these people have worked really hard for this moment and they need and deserve this final practice." He turned to face the performers: "and you know what they say in showbiz, don't you?"

They replied in unison, "The show must go on."

Brett nodded and forced a smiled. "Yes, it must," he croaked.

After the dress rehearsal, Brett walked home alone to Sea View Cottage. Robert had offered to stay with him for a while but Brett thanked him and said that he needed to be alone.

Inside the cottage, Alina's things seemed to be everywhere. Her jacket was on a peg in the hallway. Her flip-flops were under a chair. Her iPad lay on the table, two pairs of her earrings were on the mantelpiece beside a bottle of perfume and in a chair by the hearth sat Mr Tubby, a scruffy toy dog which she insisted on bringing to Cornwall because she always kept him close at hand and had done so since she had received him as a present on her sixth birthday. Brett picked up Mr Tubby and carried him into the kitchen where he sat him down on the work surface; he then poured himself a large glass of wine. The house seemed quiet. Eerily quiet and so he took both dog and wine out into the conservatory. A full moon shone through the glass roof casting shadows across the floor. He went outside and into the garden where there was hardly a breath of wind. The sweet scent of honeysuckle filled the still night air and the silence was broken only by the occasional ring of Alina's wind chimes. With glass in hand he walked to the bottom of the garden and out of the gate which led onto the coastal path. From there he went down the steps and onto the deserted beach. Slowly he walked across the sand to a bench. He sat down and placed Mr Tubby on his lap. He then took a large gulp of wine and watched as the waves tumbled gently onto the sand in the light of the clear, bright moon. He thought of Alina and how she made him laugh with her funny ways and ability to mimic even the most difficult voices and accents. But he had to confess that she had been more subdued of late. She had laughed less and at times had seemed in another world. He put it down to her work. Like so many in the acting profession work was irregular, often stressful and often in short supply. Brett finished the wine and stood the glass beside him on the bench. He leaned back with Mr Tubby clasped tightly in his arms and looked up at moon and the stars. "Why,

Alina? Why did you hurt Gideon? Why were you in the church? I don't understand."

Inside the police station, Detective Inspector Fox sat with WPC Jenkins opposite Alina and prepared to question her. She was alone on her side of the table because she refused to have a lawyer present. After telling Alina of her rights, WPC Jenkins switched on a recording machine.

At first Alina refused to co-operate but after several minutes she realised there was nothing to be achieved by keeping quiet because when all was said and done, she knew that she was guilty.

"It was not my intension to harm Gideon," she suddenly whispered, "I just needed to knock him out long enough so that I could retrieve my phone. I'd stupidly left it on the vestry floor, you see, because I panicked and ran off when I heard him call out, 'Is that you, Kitty?' Had it not been for the phone I'd have left the church and nothing further would have happened." She looked down at her hands. "Were it not for the phone no-one else would have got hurt. Gideon would not have been hurt. Hazel Mitchell would not have been hurt and nor would the poor lady in the charity shop."

"Are you implying that you were involved with some of the other crimes?"

Alina nodded. "Yes, all of them."

Detective Inspector Fox was taken aback. "All of them?"

"Yes, as I said, Gideon in the church, Hazel Mitchell at Pentrillick House and poor Maisie in the charity shop."

"But why?"

"It's a long story."

"We have all night."

"Yes, I suppose so." Alina glanced towards the window and smiled when she saw the moon. The previous evening she and Brett had walked hand in hand along the beach in the moonlight.

How things had changed in the ensuing twenty four hours! She then turned back to answer the question. "It was dusk when I fled from the church having knocked Gideon to the floor and outside I saw a woman standing at the bus stop. She turned when she heard me running and looked me in the eye. Then the bus arrived, she got on it and as it drove away it I realised that if given the opportunity she might be able to identify me although I was certain that no way would she have been able to name me."

"So you decided that you had to silence her?"

"Yes, I was worried and couldn't risk being done for GBH or whatever the charge might be. It wouldn't have been very good for my career, would it?"

"Perhaps not but how did you know who the woman you saw was?"

"I've a very good memory for faces so I did the obvious thing and went on Facebook. I typed in the names of people I knew through the drama group, hoping that whoever the woman was would be friends with one of them. I struck gold when I typed in Tess Dobson. One of her friends was Hazel Mitchell, a widow who had her occupation down as cook at Pentrillick House."

"So what did you do next?"

Alina frowned. "You know what I did."

"Yes, but I want you to tell me."

"I suggested to Brett that we went to Pentrillick House to have a look around. He thought it was a lovely idea and so we went up on Easter Monday. Once I'd fathomed out where the kitchen was I told Brett I was going to the loo and left him chatting to someone I wasn't familiar with. Hazel was in the kitchen and the window was open. It was easy."

"And afterwards?"

"I put the gun back in the small plastic bag I kept it in and then went back to Brett who was still talking so I said I'd wander down to the lake because I wanted to see the swans. He said okay and that he'd join me there shortly. I found a spot where I couldn't be seen, took the gun from the bag and threw it into the lake. The bag I screwed up and dropped into a litter bin. I then sat down on a bench and waited for Brett. And as I waited I heard the sound of sirens so knew that she had been found and was glad that there was no reason for anyone to suspect me. Of course we weren't allowed to leave until we'd all been questioned but Brett and I both said we'd heard and seen nothing nor did we know the lady who had been shot."

"And Maisie, the lady who worked in the charity shop. Where does she fit into this?"

"Ah, yes, that was rather unfortunate. You see, it suddenly occurred to me as I watched the Royal wedding, that having thrown my squeaky shoes into the box of stuff Brett had put aside for the charity shop, was rather a silly thing to have done and so I decided to try and get them back. I told Brett I was going shopping because our provisions were getting low; my intention was to call at the charity shop on my way home. However, as I got near to the shop I suddenly remembered that the two women who worked there were members of the drama group and so knew they'd recognise me. I parked in the street and hung around outside for a while wondering what to do and then to my delight I saw one of them leave the shop and walk along the main street. It was a lovely day and so the shop door was open which meant I was able to creep inside undetected. I looked around and saw a stack of pillow cases. I grabbed one and pulled it over Maisie's head and then forced her onto the floor. Unfortunately she hit her head on a stone urn that was for sale and must have knocked herself out. Next I dropped the catch on the door and turned round the sign to say 'closed'. Then to make sure she didn't get free before I'd found the shoes and made my exit, I tied up her arms and legs with scarves. Unfortunately it was all in vain because the shoes weren't there."

"No, because Marlene had already bought them."

"Sadly, yes she had." Alina frowned. "They didn't always squeak, you know. They were fine when I bought them and it wasn't until I brought them down to Cornwall they started to squeak. Silly shoes. Perhaps they didn't like the sea air."

"Okay. Let's go back to the beginning and the assault on Gideon Elms. I mean, I think I'd be very naïve if I still believed as was the case up until this afternoon, that the person who we now know to be you was looking for the silver chalice, wouldn't I?"

Alina didn't answer.

"You were looking for the items stolen from Pentrillick House a few years back, weren't you?"

Still Alina did not answer.

"You'll achieve nothing by keeping quiet, Ms Delamere other than to prolong the questioning."

Alina hung her head. "I've confessed to the assaults but have stolen nothing other than the candlesticks which I didn't want and you've got them back anyway."

"I'm not saying that you have. What I'm saying is that I believe you were trying to retrieve stolen goods which we now know were hidden in the church."

"I didn't know they had been found until this evening. It was a great shock."

"Yes, I should imagine it was."

Alina sighed. "I'm in a lot of trouble, aren't I?"

"I won't lie and say otherwise."

"And pride is one of the seven deadly sins." She hung her head.

"Pride?" Detective Inspector Fox was confused.

"Yes, you see it wasn't my intention to keep the Liddicott-Treens' things. I thought if I found them I'd leave them in situ and then pretend I'd dreamed where they were. I would tell Brett who would tell someone, probably the police or even the cute little vicar and then they'd be found. I'd be a hero. I might even receive a reward. I'd have made a name for myself."

"I see but how did you know the valuables were hidden in the church?"

Alina put her head to one side and looked at the floor.

"You've nothing to lose by naming the persons who broke into Pentrillick House," said the detective inspector, "That's assuming you know who they are."

Alina nodded. "Yes, I know. I know only too well." She took in a deep breath. "About five years ago life was tough. My acting career was going nowhere and I had a job to make ends meet. I lived in a grotty bedsit with three other girls and then I met Wade. Wade was handsome, carefree and seemed to have plenty of money. We hit it off and after a couple of months I moved in with him and everything seemed fine but then one day it occurred to me that he didn't seem to work, yet he spent money like water. I asked him how come he had money to burn but he wouldn't tell me. Then one day the coppers came round and arrested him for armed robbery. I was gutted. It turned out that he and some mates had robbed a jewellers the week before and when they made their escape the mask that one of them was wearing got caught on a hook and was pulled off. CCTV picked it up, his face was circulated and identified. He was arrested and, soon after, they came looking for Wade. They were all found guilty and received hefty prison sentences. They're still inside now. Silly sods."

"Very interesting but what does this have to do with the Pentrillick House robbery?"

"It has a lot to do with Pentrillick House because that was one of their jobs too. After they'd nicked the stuff they hid it in the church because there was a large police presence in the village that night. They intended to collect it the next day but then discovered there was a wedding on and they couldn't risk going in on Sunday because of the services. In the end they decided to leave it and come back a month or so later when the fuss had died down. Of course back then the church was left unlocked during the day for visitors to look round but since Gideon's attack it's been kept locked when not in use." She laughed in a self-mocking manner, "I rather shot myself in the foot there because it's meant I've had limited access to the building in order to search for the hidden hoard."

"I see, so Wade and his cohorts never got the chance to go back to Pentrillick because shortly after that they were arrested for the robbery at the jewellers?"

"Yes and they went to prison for that and several other crimes as well including bank robbery."

"Professionals then."

"Yes, I suppose you could call them that."

"So where were you when they burgled Pentrillick House? I assume you and Wade were an item then."

"Yes, we were but I didn't know he came to Cornwall. I was filming at the time, you see. Nothing special just a television commercial. To save travelling back and forth I stayed away for two or three nights with friends so I didn't even know that he'd been away as well."

"I see, so I take it then that after they went inside they asked you to retrieve the Liddicott-Treen's valuables knowing they couldn't do it themselves?"

Alina shook her head. "No, no, it wasn't like that at all. Wade told me about the robbery when I visited him one day and he said the stuff they'd nicked was hidden in a church in Cornwall in a village called Pentrillick. He wouldn't tell me whereabouts in the church but said when he got out he'd be a wealthy man and we'd have a good life together. Two years later I met Brett and so told Wade I wouldn't be seeing him anymore. I thought no more about the stolen goods until earlier this year when suddenly, out of the blue, Brett told me he'd bought a cottage in Cornwall. He said it would be our place in the country to escape to. When I realised it was Pentrillick I thought fate had stepped in and I vowed I'd try and find the valuables for the reasons I stated earlier. I can't believe it was under the altar. I wouldn't have looked there in a hundred years."

"Yes, a strange and cunning hiding place and I must admit I'm surprised someone like your Wade knew about the old stone altar."

"I told you, he's not my Wade, not any more but I think he might have known about it though because his dad was a clergyman so as a kid he was familiar with churches and stuff like that."

"His father was a clergyman." Detective Inspector Fox was amazed.

"Yes, but he died when Wade was a teenager. He was thirteen. A couple of years later his mother remarried. Poor Wade didn't like his stepfather and to make matters worse his stepfather didn't like him."

"And did he tell you about his father while in prison?"

"No, I already knew that bit. What I didn't know then was that it caused him to go off the rails."

Detective Inspector Fox glanced at the clock. "One more thing and then we'll wind this interview up. Where did you get the gun from?"

Alina sighed. "Again, it was Wade. Well, no, that's not quite true. He didn't actually give it to me, I found it after he was arrested amongst his stuff and I didn't know what to do with it. So when I went to visit him I mentioned it and he said, keep it, Angel, you never know when you might need it." Alina twisted the necklace she wore around her finger, "How I wish I could turn back the clock. With hindsight I realise I should have informed the police where the Liddicott-Treen's possessions were when Wade told me but I suppose if the truth be known I didn't want him to get into more trouble than he was already in."

"But had you done so you would not be sitting here opposite me now."

A tear trickled down Alina's cheek. "No, I'd be home with Brett looking forward to the opening night of his play."

Chapter Twenty Five

Murder at Mulberry Hall ran for three nights each time to a full house and on Saturday evening as the Pentrillick Players prepared for their final performance, Brett, who looked tired and pale brought a man and a woman into the dressing rooms.

"Everyone, I'd like you to meet my young brother, Alfie and his fiancée, Claire. They've come down to see the play and to give me a bit of moral support."

Alfie squeezed Brett's arm with affection. "Hi everyone. If you're half as good as Brett says you are, then we're in for a treat tonight."

Marlene stepped forward and shook hands with the young couple. "Delighted to meet you," she gushed.

Everyone else then did likewise except Hetty and Lottie who held back.

"Are you thinking what I'm thinking?" Lottie whispered.

Hetty nodded. "Yes, that's the bloke we saw on TV watching the marathon in the Mall who we thought was Brett. They're like two peas in a pod."

"Yes, and his fiancée is the girl who was with him."

"We made a bit of a bloomer there then."

"Yes, we're quite good at bloomers."

After Brett, Alfie and Claire left, the cast continued with their preparations and as with the other performances, Hetty had the sprig of white heather safely tucked inside the pocket of her apron.

"Ten minutes to go," called Robert when he came back stage to make sure all was well, "and there's a real party atmosphere out there tonight."

As he left, Ginny who was prompter approached Hetty and Lottie and smiled. "I see your girls have a new friend. I think that's really sweet."

The sisters were nonplussed.

"Who's that then?" Lottie asked.

"Lucky Lucy Lacey," smiled Ginny, "they're out there in the audience together and Lucy is sitting between Kate and Vicki. It looks like they're enjoying a good natter."

"That's right," said Maisie, "and Lucy's wearing the dress she bought recently. It's lovely to see the old girl so happy."

"Hey, less of the old," tutted Daisy, "she's only a few years older than us."

"So how come your twins know Lucy?" Tess asked.

"They went to her cottage to buy lucky heather during the Easter holiday," said Lottie, "but I don't think they've seen her since."

Emma chuckled as she placed her housemaid's cap over her dark hair. "Actually Zac told me they're friends on Facebook and have been since Easter so they've been in touch quite a lot since then."

"Lucy has the internet!" Lottie was flabbergasted.

"Yes, she had it installed after her mother died so that she didn't feel quite so isolated," stated Ginny, "I remember her telling me about it in the post office a few years back."

After the final performance the entire production team went to the Crown and Anchor for celebration drinks and a buffet which Tristan Liddicott-Treen who, together with his family had been in the audience, insisted on paying for.

"Champagne," gasped Tess, when Alison the landlady produced bottles from the chiller.

"I think you all deserve it," remarked Tristan, "I don't think I've laughed so much for ages."

"Nor me," agreed his wife, Samantha, "you all get better every year."

Outside on the sun terrace, Hetty and Lottie sat with Kitty. "I can't believe it's all over," Hetty sighed. She looked downcast. "I don't think I've had so much fun for many a year. Everything will feel very flat tomorrow, especially when the children have gone home."

"And not only is the play finished but the all mysteries have been solved too so we'll have nothing at all to focus on now." Lottie also looked sorrowful.

Hetty suddenly laughed. "Hmm, but it's probably just as well that the mysteries have been solved because we were about as much use as a chocolate teapot. Talk about barking up the wrong tree on all three accounts."

Lottie tilted her head to one side. "Not directly but we were still involved and remember it was you, Hetty, who suggested the church be painted. Were it not for that then the Liddicott-Treens' belongings would not have been found."

"True, although it was your granddaughter who suggested moving the altar," Hetty reminded her.

"Yes, I'm very proud of her for that."

"Although I must admit I was surprised to hear her say she'd helped decorate the church back home."

"I'm not," said Lottie, "They had a new rector in the village a few years back and he started a youth club. Kate used to go, well she probably still does, and it must have been the youth club members who helped prepare to decorate the church."

"Does or did Vicki go as well?" Kitty asked.

"No, she said it wasn't her thing," Lottie laughed, "You can't get Vicki to do what she doesn't want to do."

Hetty smiled. "So I've noticed and she sometimes reminds me of a young me."

"I'm not going to disagree with that," smiled Lottie as she drained her champagne glass, "and funnily enough she's joined the St John's Ambulance as a cadet just as you did. Sandra told me when they were here for Easter but I think you were out walking Albert at the time and I forgot to tell you."

Kitty wagged her finger. "And another thing, Het. You put the police onto Alina after you saw her in church but being a damn good actress she convinced them her visit was innocent."

"Very good point," acknowledged Hetty.

"Poor Brett," sighed Lottie, "I think it was very brave of him to stay on to see the performances through but I fear *Murder at Mulberry Hall* will always leave a nasty taste in his mouth."

"Yes, he's hidden his feelings well these last few days and I should imagine the magnitude of it all hasn't even hit him yet." Hetty glanced over to where Brett stood talking to his brother.

"Do you think they were very close?" Kitty asked, "Brett and Alina that is?"

"You never can tell," said Hetty, "but judging by the strained look in his eyes I'd say that he was pretty fond of her."

As her words faded, Penelope Prendergast came out onto the terrace. "Ah there you are, ladies. Just wanted to say how much we enjoyed the show. What a hoot and we're really proud of our Sammy. And that inspector chappie had us in stitches."

"Yes, that'll be Sid," chuckled Hetty, "He's a real character."

Penelope sat down on a nearby chair. "Now, before you go you must have another box of broken biscuits. We've loads in the car and haven't had a chance to give any out yet because we didn't get here until last night."

"Perhaps we can pick them up from the Vicarage tomorrow," suggested Lottie, "save you going out to the car now and save us carrying them home."

"Yes, that would be a much better idea and you must have a box too, Kitty."

"Thank you, Penelope. That'll keep Tommy happy."

"Jolly good. We go home tomorrow but I'll unpack them all before we go and leave them with Sammy."

While Zac played pool, Emma asked Vicki and Kate who sat with Lucy, what they wanted to do when they left school.

Zac looked up from the pool table and laughed. "That's simple, Em. Right now they both want to be vicar's wives and not just any old vicar." He nodded towards Vicar Sam who was talking to Robert and Paul.

"Actually," said Kate, "after all the excitement of these past few days and the fact that someone predicted I'd be one," She smiled at Lucy, "I've decided I'm definitely going to be a police officer."

"Are you really?" Vicki asked.

"Yes, and I'm serious. I mean, had it not been for me suggesting the altar be pulled out then the valuable stuff would never have been found."

"But that doesn't mean you'd be any good at solving crimes," laughed Vicki.

"No, but it's a start."

"So, are you going to be a history teacher, Vicki?" Lucy asked, with a twinkle in her eye.

Vicki scowled. "I hope not. Perhaps you ought to read my broken biscuit again, Lucy. I mean, it could be that a crumb broke off and changed the shape or something like that."

Much to the surprise of those around Lucy began to laugh and she laughed until the tears rolled down her cheeks.

"What's so funny?" Vicki asked, finding herself smiling due to the infectious laughter.

"Your face, dear. You should see it," Lucy composed herself. "I'm sorry but I've been having you on. I knew you strongly disliked history, you see, and that's why I chose it as a future occupation. I'll be truthful now and believe you will become a nurse and you'll marry a doctor."

Vicki's jaw dropped. "But…but…how did you know I've an interest in nursing?"

"I just do."

"And the broken biscuits?" Kate asked, "Can you really read them?"

Lucy shook her head. "No, no of course not. I can see certain things in the future but biscuits play no part." She looked a little sheepish. "When you get the chance please tell your aunt I was pulling her leg. You see, when I was seven years old my grandmother pretended to read my fortune with the aid of a broken biscuit much to the amusement of my parents. She confessed later and I saw the funny side but that memory has stuck with me over the years. When your aunt bought a sprig of heather and then kindly offered me a cup of tea, for some reason I felt a little impish and so when she produced the biscuits I pulled my grandmother's trick. Her face was a picture but please tell her I'm sorry."

"But what you told her came true," said Vicki.

"Yes, yes, it did but I can assure you that it was nothing to do with the broken biscuit."

Kate laughed. "Grandma will be in stitches when we tell her because she told Auntie Het she was gullible to believe in lucky heather and fortune telling."

Lucy tutted. "Now don't you knock my heather."

"Oh, I won't," said Kate, "I have great faith in it. In fact I have every intention of having it with me when I take my exams."

"Me too," concurred Vicki.

Lucy bit her bottom lip. "I shall miss you both when you've gone home. You've given me a new lease of life and I feel twenty years younger. I appreciate that."

Vicki sighed. "Yes, and sadly we go home tomorrow."

"But I'm sure we'll be back again before the year is out," reflected Kate, "We might even be able to persuade Mum and Dad to come down for Christmas."

As Zac was about to endorse Vicki's proposal, he noticed a boy and a girl who looked a little a little younger than himself watching the game of pool.

"Fancy a game in a minute?" Zac asked.

"Yes, please," said the boy eagerly.

The girl shook her head.

When the game finished, Zac handed a pool cue to the boy. "I'm Zac. Zac Burton."

"Thank you, Zac. I'm Jeremy. Jeremy Liddicott-Treen and this is my sister Jemima."

"Ah, so you're from Pentrillick House."

"That's right. We don't come in here very often but tonight's special because we've been to see the play which I thought was brilliant."

"So did I," added Jemima.

"Yes, I thought it was pretty good too," admitted Zac. He started to set up the pool balls. "Is there any more news regarding your cook?"

A broad grin crept across Jeremy's face. "Yes, she's doing really, really well. My father took me to visit her today because she wanted to see me," Jeremy laughed, "You see, before she was shot I told her about a book I'd started to read and she wanted to know how it ended and whether the person I thought was a confidence trickster actually was."

"And was he?" Zac asked.

"You bet. When I told Mrs Mitchell she laughed and then she cried."

"That's because she knew someone called Andrew Banks who was a crook," hissed Jemima, with scorn.

"I know he was a crook," smiled Jeremy, "but Mrs Mitchell saw the good in him which doesn't surprise me because she's like that."

"You were brilliant tonight, Hetty," gushed Debbie, "I don't think I've laughed so much for ages."

"Thank you."

"I'll second that," said Tess, having heard Debbie's comment.

"And you were good as well, Tess," Debbie added, "In fact you were all good."

"Thank you and I don't think I'd be exaggerating if I said we on the stage enjoyed it as much as you in the audience did."

Hetty felt quite choked and so changed the subject. "Who's that chap over there with Marlene's husband, Gary?"

"He's a real hunk, isn't he?" Tess giggled.

"Yes, I suppose he is but I was asking more out of curiosity."

"Oh, I see. He's Gary's brother and he and his wife came over tonight to watch the play. That's his wife over there talking to Marlene. The woman in the pretty red dress."

The sisters looked across the room to where Marlene stood talking to several women.

"Any idea of his name?" Lottie asked, as something suddenly occurred to her.

"Andrew," said Tess, "and don't tell anyone, but Marlene told me that she and Andrew are organising a surprise birthday party for Gary's fiftieth at the end of the month. Isn't that sweet?"

Debbie blushed as Tess returned to her husband who was beckoning her. "Oh dear. No doubt he's the Andrew that Marlene was on the phone to a week or so ago in the back garden and it turns out he's her brother-in-law. What a Charlie I am."

"Well, I think between us we've all made quite a few errors this summer," admitted Hetty, "I certainly have but hopefully no-one got hurt by any of them."

"There is still one more end to tie up," Lottie reminded them, "I'm referring to Marlene's meeting with the same chap on Tuesday nights who we know wasn't Andrew Banks."

"Oh dear," Hetty groaned, "I don't think I want to know what that was all about."

Debbie nodded. "I'm inclined to agree."

A little later Robert announced that the food was laid out in the dining room.

Hetty rubbed her hands together. "Good, because I'm actually quite peckish."

When they entered the dining room, Tess and Marlene were already at the buffet table.

"Now the play is over I can concentrate on our holiday," said Tess, as she placed spiced chicken wings on a plate, "hubby and me are off to Spain at the end of August. I would say in search of the sun but with the summer we're currently having that might not be necessary."

"Really," said Marlene, "Gary and I intend to go there with the children next year because by then I should be able to speak Spanish like a native."

"You're having lessons then." Tess was impressed.

"Yes, every Tuesday I go to Penzance for classes. I really enjoy them and it's very handy because one of our class members lives in Helston and so he picks me up on the way to save me driving. They're a smashing group of people and sometime after the meeting we pop into a pub and converse in Spanish." She laughed. "Goodness knows what the locals must think."

Hetty heard what was said. Her cheeks turned pink. "I never wanted to be a detective anyway," she whispered, as Tess and Marlene moved away from the buffet table.

"Me neither," agreed Lottie, "Knitting is much more up my street."

"And I'll stick to gardening," Hetty dropped a pickled gherkin onto her plate. "In fact when we get home I shall tear up our suspect list."

"So that's the end of our investigations then?"

Hetty smiled. "Yes, until the next time."

THE END

Printed in Great Britain
by Amazon